Hidden Scion

HILLSIDE KINGS BOOK FIVE
BOOK FIVE

CARMEN ROSALES

Carmen Rosales
Copyright © 2023 by Carmen Rosales
Cover Design © 2023 by 3Crows Author Services

Erotic Quill Publishing, LLC
3020 NE 41st Terrace STE 9 #243
Homestead, Fl. 33033

www.carmenrosales.com

Editing by Heartfullofreads

Manufactured in the United States of America
First Edition June 2023
ISBN 978-1-959888-24-6

Also by Carmen Rosales

Hillside Kings Series

Hidden Scars

Hidden Lies

Hidden Secrets

Hidden Truths

Hidden Scion

Entre Familia: Cartel Kings

Cartel Kings book one 1/16/2024

Cartel Kings book two-coming soon

Cartel book three-coming soon

Cartel Kings book four-coming soon

A Dark Duet

Giselle

Briana

Standalone's

Dirty Little Secrets-Coming Soon

Dearly Beloved-Coming Soon

Vows Written in Blood-Coming Soon

Hidden Ties

Like A Moth To A Flame-Coming Soon

The Prey Series

Thirst

Lust

Appetite

Forgive Me For I Have Sinned-Coming Soon

Steamy Romance

Changing the Game

Until Her

Until Now

To my husband, thank you for inspiring me to write the Hillside Kings Series and for all your support.

Sometimes a love is so great and so big that all we can do is hold on to it forever.

CARMEN ROSALES

Trigger Warning

Dear Reader,

The is a dark romance. The list of triggers include abuse, death, and acts of violence.

Welcome to Hillside

cho·lo

/ˌCHōlō/

noun: cholo; plural noun: cholos

a young man belonging to a Mexican American urban subculture associated with street gangs.

cho·la

/ˌCHōlə/

a young woman belonging to a Mexican American urban subculture associated with street gangs.

cabrón

(Mexico) (= amigo) hey, you! (=malo)

¡cabrón! you bastard! (very informal)

muñeca

means "doll" This term can be used to either playfully indicate the woman is pretty.

hyna

A hispanic slam term for a Mexican female mostly used by Cholos (gangsters)

culazo

AZO/AZA termination means by generally large, butt

Sabes qué

You know what? Or Guess what?
hijo de la chingada
Means son of a bitch
mi Reina
My queen
payaso
Clown
Vato/holmes
Guy or dude
carnal/carnalita
friend
Ese
Dude/bro/homie
pinche pendejo (man)/pinche pendeja(woman)
Fucking asshole

All characters and names of gangs are fictional and created by the author. Please note that the Hillside Kings Series is not affiliated to any gang, cartel, or member.

Preface

**Their love was forbidden from the start.
Now he has to do everything he can to save it.**

Alex Cortez is used to putting his life on the line as the Hidden Scion of the Cortez cartel. But when he is charged with the protection of his best friend's sister and her son, he braces himself to bury old feelings deep. Alina is off-limits, stubborn and gorgeous, but Alex is torn by the secret he has kept for all these years——their one forbidden night marked him forever.

Alina Flores is in trouble. On the run from her abusive ex, she's collided head-on with her past. Now, she has to accept protection from the only man who ever broke her heart——the man she swore she'd never see again. But as Alex becomes part of her day-to-day, *again*, things heat up, tempers flare, and feelings Alina thought were long buried start to surface.

Alex keeps telling himself he did the right thing by ghosting her, but when Alina's secrets are revealed, his world turns upside down. Except this time, he's not the one walking away...

HIDDEN SCION *is a steamy, open-door standalone featuring Alex Cortez of the East Hillside Kings and his childhood love who stole his heart. Guaranteed HEA.*

xiv

One

ALINA

"You may now kiss the bride."

My heart melts every time I hear this part at a wedding. The part that solidifies a union with a single kiss.

When Leo raises Katalia's veil and leans in to kiss her, there's a split second of silence. A second of silence where you could hear a pin drop before everyone erupts in cheers. It's that second you take it all inside. The reason, the love, and the promise of a future. It's that second where you wonder if you could ever love a person that much or if a person could love you the same way in return. Some people have been lucky to find it, and some still have hope they will one day.

Then there are those like me. Bystanders living in the real world full of lust and hate. Living the consequences of their mistakes or maybe their fate. Where there is no love by a significant other; only pain and loneliness.

My heart warms when Leo and Katalia smile ~~to~~ at their friends and family. Everyone's here—my brother, members of the Kings, Leo's friends and family.

"Can I go play now, Mom?"

I look down at my pride and joy. "Yes, baby, but make sure it's not too far and where I can see you, okay?"

My five-year-old son, Maximus, nods, then runs over to a group of kids playing by the grass.

The wedding is on the back patio of Leo and Katalia's newly built mansion located in the West of Hillside close to their family. It must be nice to live like the rich and famous, but I know it comes at a price. The price that everyone has to overlook. The sacrifice of blood, sweat, and tears—drugs, dead bodies, and lies.

The sons and daughters of cartel leaders don't have a choice. They are born and bred in this type of lifestyle.

My brother, Joaquin, steps close and asks, "Are you okay?"

He's dressed up in a nice tux compared to my fifty-five-dollar TJ Maxx dress. Katalia invited me at the last minute, and I couldn't refuse. She has been so welcoming to me and Maxim. Not to mention, her little brother and Maxim get along ever since they met at the county fair a few weeks ago.

"Yeah, it's a beautiful wedding."

He nods with a hopeful expression. "One day, it will be you getting married, wearing a beautiful dress."

I plaster a fake smile on my face. "Girls like me don't have fairy-tale weddings, *hermano*."

"You think that because you trusted the wrong person, gave them a son, and they hurt you. But that is all on me for not paying attention and for not protecting you like I promised I would," he croaks out.

He blames himself for what happened to me when I got involved with Joker. If he only knew who was to blame. I should have known better than to get involved with a King.

"It's not your fault, *hermano*. To be honest, I got the best thing out of it."

He nods. His expression softens when he watches his nephew. "Are you sure you will be okay staying with Smiley? Promise to not give him a hard time, eh?"

The mention of Smiley or anything to do with Alex Cortez has a fire building in the pit of my stomach like my own internal hell.

"As long as he stays out of my way. But you know how Smiley is;

he has his way of doing things that irritates me. Ever since I arrived, he thinks I'm a child and treats me like I can't take care of myself."

"He's just being overprotective because he knows you are in trouble and you're like family, *hermanita*. It's not his fault. I asked him to watch over you and my nephew."

Joaquin smiles and shifts on his feet. The tiny hairs on my arms stand up. I swear I can smell him before I can even see him. It doesn't matter what cologne he wears. It mixes with his manly scent, making it his own signature scent that screams I'm here.

It's intoxicating. The more you inhale it, the more you want, like an addiction that therapy couldn't fix.

My brother nods at him and says, "Looking good, Carnal. You clean up nice."

My eyes finally land on the man who stole my heart at seventeen, only to break it twenty-four hours later. He looks like a tattooed model in a tailored tux. Broad shoulders, sharp jaw, short hair shaved on the sides.

I thought he was good-looking when I first arrived at his doorstep a few weeks ago, but nothing prepared me for this version of him. A cartel boss. The kind you see in the movies. Powerful and sophisticated.

His father is Mason's uncle which makes them cousins, and when I learned that Smiley fell in love with Luciana, Mason's wife, before they got married, I was devastated. I decided to bury my feelings for him and found that hating him was better than being heartbroken and feeling sorry for myself for not being good enough for him.

"So do you, carnal," Alex responds.

"You ever going to join the guys in married life?"

My heart pounds and my palms sweat. I try to avert my gaze, but I'm frozen, waiting to hear his response. He hasn't acknowledged my presence. Apparently, for Alex, I'm invisible.

Alex sighs. "Damn, *ese*. You know how I feel about marriage. I've thought about it, but the life I lead has no room for a wife and kids."

I know deep in my heart that I was never part of his plan.

I never was.

I'm about to turn and find Maximus, but I guess today is the day I need to remind myself all the reasons why Alex Cortez will never see me more than his best friend's little sister.

"Hey, *preciosa*. You look beautiful," Alex says to Luciana as she walks toward us with a soft smile.

Luciana is beautiful, rich, powerful, and everything I'm not. A cartel princess who is now a queen. Any guy would be crazy not to want her. She's perfect.

"Thank you," she replies in a soft voice.

My clammy hands slide down my dress as if that's going to change the fact that it looks cheap compared to her beautiful white lace dress that cinches at the waist, flaring out at the hip, and matching pointed pumps.

I blink back the sting behind my eyes, hating myself for caring so much. It must be the wedding and the emotions that events like this invoke. Like the fact that no one has ever told me I looked beautiful and meant it.

Luciana turns to me with a bright smile, and as much as I want to hate her, I can't.

She doesn't know.

No one knows I slept with Alex once, and it was only because I asked him to. He didn't force me, but he didn't deny me either. Back then, I was a stupid girl who was saving herself for her crush and practically begged him.

"Alina, right?" Luciana asks.

"Yeah."

"It's nice that you could make it and I could finally meet you in person. When I visited L.A., Joaquin always talked about you."

I grin. "All good things, I hope."

"He always said you were busy being a good mom."

"I try."

Like right now. I'm trying not to fall apart.

Two

ALINA

After promising Joaquin I would call, I walk up the pathway to Alex's house with Maxim in tow. After two hours of playing with the kids out on the patio, I was relieved he wanted to go to Alex's house to relax.

It gave me the excuse to leave. Staying with Alex in his house makes me feel like a failure. In my mind, it has always been me and Maxim against the world. My brother doesn't count because his focus is on the Hillside Kings in L.A. As for Danny, he thought I was his sex toy and a punching bag. It didn't start out that way of course.

I chose to move out on my own even with L.A.'s crazy rent prices after I gave birth to Maxim when Danny promised it was the best thing for me and the baby. He knew I didn't want to raise him with a bunch of gangbangers in and out of the house. He assured me that he would help out if I moved from my brother's house because it wasn't safe to raise a child there, but not everyone tells the truth.

I'm about to knock but then I remember I have the key even though there is a keypad at the door.

I open my bag looking for the key mentally telling myself I should have put it on the key ring so it's easier to find when awareness snakes up my spine and the man that is causing it sticks his hand out punching in the code hearing the door beep and the bolt of the lock slide open.

"It's five oh four three," Alex whispers.

Maxim looks up with a megawatt smile on his face. "Hi, Smiley."

Ever since winning him the fishes at the county fair a couple of weeks ago, Alex is his favorite person.

"Hey, Maxim," Alex greets him with a smile. "Do you want to feed the fish? I still have them in the glass bowl we put them in."

Maxim makes a face when he looks at his clothes. "I think I want to change first."

"Yeah, *chavalito*. That's a is a good idea. Go, get changed and I'll wait for you in the living room."

Maxim takes off to the spare guest room next to Alex's room.

"Thank you," I tell him while he waits for me to enter his house.

"He's a good kid. You've done a good job with him, considering..."

He means Danny. Although it's a compliment, I sense the judgment in his voice.

"Considering what?"

He closes the door and takes a deep breath while he takes off his suit jacket. "Considering that his father is a *pinchy cabron* that beats his mom. That's what. Why did you stay with him, huh? I'm sure it wasn't the first time, Alina."

Actually, I never lived with Danny. He would show up after sweet-talking me when I was at my lowest. Alex left me vulnerable, and I was young and stupid. That's when Danny came along. After I had Maxim, his true colors popped up and spread like a wildfire.

Alex moved with his sister to Arizona and was never around, and my brother was too busy to notice. After Ramon supposedly died and they made Alex the leader of the East Hillside Kings, Danny got worse. He despised being pushed aside.

Danny even threatened to kill me if I said anything about the way he treated me. So, I stayed silent and suffered. He went rogue, heading off to Mexico. Word on the street is that he's a sicario—a hitman for the Mexican cartels.

Him being a sicario has helped him. The last time I saw him was two months ago when he left me unconscious on my kitchen floor after I threatened to tell Joaquin about his whereabouts and what he's into.

Maxim was able to call his uncle from my cellphone, and Joaquin had rushed me to the hospital. Before he left, he promised he'd come back for me, that no matter how far I ran, it'd be futile.

The cops didn't do anything because it was a gang conflict.

"What the fuck do you care, huh? You don't give a shit about me. The only reason I'm here is because of a favor my brother asked of you."

Alex pinches his nose and closes his eyes. "You know what? Forget it. It's none of my business. I have no right to question you. I just thought you were smarter than that."

I scoff. "You're right." I step closer, and he retreats. "You don't know shit." I point down the hall where Maxim is out of earshot and lower my voice. "Everything I do, whether you think it's right or wrong, is for my son. I'm here because my brother begged me to come."

"I'm not judging you, Alina, but if you would have said something sooner, it wouldn't have gotten this out of hand."

"Would you have rescued me, Smiley? If Joaquin hadn't found out, would you have checked up on me and my son? Called me?"
Silence.
Exactly.
He hasn't spoken to me in over five years. To Alex, I'm a memory he's been trying to erase. I'm the dirty secret. It just hurts to know I mean so little to someone I fell in love with.

"Look, I'm sorry. I overstepped."
Maxim races down the hallway. "Smiley! I'm ready."
Alex rolls up the sleeves of his shirt tearing his eyes away from me, revealing his inked forearms. He has gotten more since I last saw him. Cholos in the Chicano culture have tattoos, but those signify a

memory, an event, a birth, a death. New loves and lost loves. It's personal. Unique to their style and beliefs. It's a culture. *La cultura*.

Alex opens the wood cabinet where he keeps the fish food and holds it out to Maxim.

My heart aches because the only man that has been nice to Maxim is his uncle. Alex takes the time to listen, and when Maxim asks for something, he checks in with me first to make sure it is okay.

"Mom?"

I smile. "Yes, my love?"

The room goes quiet while he continues to watch the goldfish eating the flakes in the glass bowl. "You look pretty today."

It was like my son was listening to the thoughts in my head at the wedding while my heart rattled inside my chest.

At just five, my son amazes me with the things he says, and it makes all my sacrifices worth it. He's worth it. I couldn't imagine my life without him in it.

"I didn't hear anyone tell you. I promised, remember? Everyone looked nice at the wedding, but you are the prettiest."

My heart swells with emotion.

"That's why you're my prince. I love you, Maxim. *Sabes que*, do you want me to make you enchiladas or pancakes? I'll be back late, and I want to make sure you eat before dropping you off with Esperanza."

Esperanza is Hector's wife and she has been helping me babysit Maxim while I work at night.

Maxim whips his head when I offer to make one of his favorite dishes. "Isn't it too late for breakfast?"

I scrunch up my nose and grin. "Says who?"

He shrugs his shoulders. "I don't know. I thought you could only eat pancakes at breakfast time."

"If my son wants pancakes, he gets pancakes. Who cares when it's served."

He smiles, his dimple popping out. "You're the best, mom."

My eyes lift to Alex with the brown container of fish food in his hand. His gaze travel down my dress as if he's looking at me for the first time. My insides flutter, but I know better than to be carried away.

The love I have bottled inside will never be reciprocated and will always remain unrequited.

Shaking off my thoughts, I walk toward the bedroom and continue to plan the rest of my life without Alex Cortez in it.

Three

ALEX

What do you do when the woman you are attracted to hates you? You act like she isn't torturing you with her smile and her perfect body. The only attention you can give her without making it obvious is to bestow it on her perfect son, Maxim.

The worst part is that you have to keep it a secret from everyone, including your best friend that trusted you with his family.

When Joaquin asked me to protect his sister and his nephew, alarm bells rang in my ears, but then I told myself that what happened between us was years ago. It's all in the past. She moved on, and so did I. How bad could it be to have her live with me for a while?

Yes, I slept with her in high school. It was one night. It was perfect, but I couldn't face my best friend without ghosting her. I know it was a shitty thing to do to her, but I didn't know how to deal with the look in her eyes when I was inside her or the way she moaned my name. I wasn't ready for all the emotions she stirred inside me.

I was selfish.

There was no way in hell I would turn her down and let some

asshole touch her for her first time. I made sure I made it good for her, but I knew I had crossed a line after it was over.

Joaquin had one rule when it came to his sister—not to fuck her behind his back. And that is exactly what I did.

I was young, weak. She was gorgeous, and the rest was history. There isn't a moment I try to tell myself it was a mistake, but I knew better. The same way I know better now. I don't regret it though.

It probably makes me a bad friend, but there are worse assholes out there, and his name is Joker. He beat the shit out of her and I'm sure it has been going on for a while.

When I catch that motherfucker; he will wish he never laid on eyes on her.

I place the fish food away after catching myself for gawking her and mentally kicking myself for not telling her she looked nice. I practically dismissed her in front of Luciana. I feel like a total dick, but I guess it's better this way. I was too hung up on hiding the elephant in the room in front of Joaquin and wasn't thinking straight. I was too busy ignoring Alina by using Lucy as a distraction.

Luciana was never mine to begin with. It doesn't change the fact that I fell in love with her. But as soon as it began, it was over, and I had to get over her the same way I did with Alina—sleep with someone else and move on.

A knock on the door breaks me out of my stupor, and I open it to find Julio and Carlito.

"What's up, *holmes*?" Julio greets me with a smile. They have been running with me since the incident with Katalia and her ex-psycho boyfriend.

Carlito nudges his head at me and notices Maxim. "He loves the fish, eh?"

"Orale."

"He's a good-looking kid. He looks just like his mom," Julio adds.

My eyes flick to Julio. He's not wrong. But he definitely finds her attractive enough to mention *good-looking*.

Julio looks at his shoes when I keep watching him. My eyes flick to Carlito, but he is too busy looking at the fishes with Maxim. A door from the hallway opens and closes behind me just then.

Awareness washes over Julio's face, and I don't miss the way his eyes follow Alina when she walks in the room or that I'm annoyed by the fact he is enjoying what he sees.

I can't blame him for checking her out; Alina has straight jet-black hair, sexy tattoos on her arms, perfect breasts, and ass for days with a cinched waist. A small straight nose and a perfect smile. The fact that she has a kid only adds to her appeal. A man that notices her knows what he gets after she has your kid—the perfect mother for your child and a beautiful woman to spend your life with. She just picked the wrong guy.

Now that she chose to leave him and run, it means she needs protection, but it also means she is available. They weren't married, according to Joaquin. The fucker didn't ask and she sure as hell didn't have a ring on her finger.

I turn just in time as she walks in the kitchen in black leggings that look like they are painted on the globes of her perfect ass and a loose off-the-shoulder t-shirt.

When Maxim follows his mother to the kitchen, eager for his pancakes, I stick my arm out, stopping Julio from following Maxim.

His head turns in surprise, but I keep my voice low. "Be careful, *ese*. She isn't some *hyna* you can mess with. Alina is off-limits. She's Joaquin's sister and that means she's family."

"I was just going to say hi, Smiley. I wasn't trying to overstep."

Carlito leans close to Julio, and in a low voice, says, "I would be careful, *ese*. Alina doesn't fuck around. She's grown up with the Kings in L.A. If you think you're the first *vato* to step up to her..." He snorts and continues, "You better have steel balls, because Alina will cut them off."

I chuckle. Alina can be a real bitch when the mood strikes. I just wish she wasn't with me.

Four

ALINA

"Damn Dulce, are you ever going to give lap dances?" Jade asks behind me in the back dressing room of the strip club. Jade has caramel-colored skin and honey-colored eyes. She doesn't do drugs or sell her pussy for money. She does give private dances, and that is as far as she goes.

I was looking for work when I moved to Arizona and wasn't planning on dancing at the Satin Doll strip club, but when the school emailed me the bill for my next class, I knew there was no way an hourly job would cut it.

Dulce is my stage name. It has been the same since I turned eighteen and started to dance for money back in L.A. It was the only way I could afford my apartment.

"No, sweetheart," I reply, checking my makeup in the dressing mirror. "It's my only rule. No lap dances or paid sex. I dance, and that's it."

She shakes her head. "You could be making so much more money with lap dances. I get the sex part. We aren't prostitutes," she says, then pauses when one of the girls walks in half-naked behind us. Jade looks at Bambi through the mirror and then continues, "Well, some of us."

Bambi is blonde with blue eyes and has a petite body that guys

15

go crazy over, but I think it's more the fact that word gets around that she is a sure thing for the right price. She says she is okay with it, but I know better. There is nothing okay when a guy sees you as a piece of meat with no feelings and uses you because they know you need the money. The men that come in here are usually...not nice.

But that doesn't stop her. Bambi gives all exotic dancers a bad name. She fucks for money and she doesn't care as long as the price is right. It's probably why she drives a late model of BMW and I drive an old Toyota Camry.

After I finish my degree in marketing from the online program at UCLA, I could get something better and start the rest of my life with my son.

I'm hoping I could make enough for Maxim to start West Hillside Elementary instead of the public school in the east.

"Are you two talking about me again?" Bambi pouts.

I try to stifle in my laugh. "Nah, we just live to watch you dance when all that money gets thrown at you."

"You could make more, Dulce. You have the looks and body. Do you know how many guys come up to me asking if you would give them a private dance?"

I roll my eyes. "I don't want to know and I don't care. Those are my rules."

I laid the rules out thick when I applied to dance here. I don't feel comfortable with some guy's creepy hands all over me. I have had enough with the blows I received from Danny.

"I have been telling her this, Bambi, but homegirl won't listen," Jade adds, closing the top of the lipstick she just used.

"It's your turn, love. It's time to show the boys what they can't have," Bambi says, winking at me.

On stage, I grab a sanitizing sheet and wipe down the metal pole, hearing cat-calls and hollering sounds from the crowd.

It's Thursday night, and it's a full house. I scan the faces, seeking one person to fixate on to get me through my set.

It makes the process easier, because being topless with nipple pasties and a thong in a room full of men and women takes a certain type of bravery.

Jade walks up behind the curtain right before my set is about to start. I try once more to find my mark for the night but spot a familiar face. I think his name is Julio, a member of the East Hillside Kings.

He's funny and nice.

I've only interacted with him at the fair, but he's the safest bet tonight.

But then, I haven't gotten around to tell Alex about where I work exactly. Our conversations are anything but chatty. Either Julio has a death wish for following me here or Alex asked him to. If it was the latter, he probably wanted me to notice a tatted *cholo* inside a strip club with a huge crown tattoo that reads Hillside Kings. There are no other members or Alex around.

My stomach clenches because this man's going to see me practically naked.

For the first time in a long while, shame spreads up my body, but I push it down.

I can do this.

Jade comes up behind me and says, "Come on, Dulce. I requested a bad bitch song for your set and everything."

I take a deep breath and nod, knowing there's no way out of this.

I can do this.

Five

ALEX

As I wait for Carlito and seven members of the East Hillside Kings to finish loading the bags of cash inside the trunk of my car, I check my phone every few seconds for a message to come through from Julio.

The drop was simple. We sold guns and had them funneled through Mexico by the Kings' cartel families so that they can be sold. It's a dirty business, but someone has to do it. If not, shit gets out of hand which leads to people dying.

Mexico is not like the U.S. where Narcos can walk a local store and purchase guns. They need to obtain them in the black market where they are not traced by the government.

My phone buzzes in my pocket, and I slide it out.

Julio: I followed Alina to work like you wanted me to. You're not going to like where she has been working these past few weeks.

I asked Julio to follow Alina for safety reasons. I wanted to be the one to do it, but I needed to be here tonight and didn't have much of a choice. She needs protection, and Julio was the better choice out of the guys that were with me tonight. He has a good aim with a gun and he always has his phone on him. Sometimes, I think the *vato* sleeps with it next to his ear or some shit.

Me: Where?

Julio: Dancing at the Satin Doll strip club.

I read the text. Then, re-read it again just in case I'm too high from the last hit of my joint. I close my eyes as anger unfurls inside of me.

What the actual fuck! Fuck, Alina.

I slam my hand on my steering wheel right when Carlito slides inside the front passenger seat of my black 1970 Plymouth Roadrunner.

Me: I'll be right there.

"What's wrong, Smiley?" Carlito asks.

"*Sabes que*, we have to head to the Satin Doll so I can knock some sense into this *chavala's* head and drag her out of there."

"What *chavala*?"

Annoyed, I say her name, as his eyebrows raise to his hairline.

"She dances at a strip club?"

"No, *pinche cabron*. She sells tacos. Yes, she is dancing at a strip club. Julio is watching her as we speak," I respond sarcastically.

Julio better not be looking too hard or I'll have to stab him in the eyes. The thought of what she is wearing or not wearing at all has my blood boiling. How could she? Out of all the fucking things to do, she has to fucking dance at a strip club for money.

I wonder if Joaquin knows what she's been up to because I'm positive this isn't her first rodeo.

I drive for twenty minutes toward the Satin Doll strip club. I treat the members of Hillside Kings here often when they are celebrating a birthday or something. But, I don't pay for pussy.

The thought of Alina doing more than just dancing pops in my head, and I push on the brakes harder than necessary when pulling into a parking space.

"Damn, *ese*. Is it that big of a deal?" Carlito asks, holding himself from flying forward with the palm of his hand on the black dashboard.

The murderous look on my face has him scurrying out.

"Alright, *patron*. I get it."

I push open the car door and step out, pulling my black hoodie over my head, while the rest of the members pull up next to us. "Get what?" I snap.

Carlito has his forearms on the hood of the car when he looks at me with a worried expression. "I know it's Joaquin's sister and you guys are close, but I see the way you look at her, carnal. The way you two are always at each other's throats. Is there something we should know?"

I hate having to lie about the past and how I truly feel about Alina.

"No. There's nothing you should know. Joaquin is my boy. He's been there for me and is loyal to the Kings. He asked me to protect his sister and that is what we will do. She's like a sister to me and no one wants to see their sister dancing at a club like this. We can't protect her like this, and if she thinks we are going to sit here and allow her to risk her life when that piece of shit is out there, she has another thing coming. For that, she should have stayed in L.A."

"Alright, *ese*. You have a point," Carlito responds with a nod.

⋯⭒👑⭒⋯

The owner of the Satin Doll spots me as soon as I walk inside with the Kings in tow.

"You boys celebrating tonight?" Tomas says with a smile.

"Nah, I'm looking for someone."

He frowns, eyeing me nervously. "Are they in the crowd? Do you need me to escort them out? You know I hate trouble, Alex. It's bad for business."

"I'm here for a woman named Alina. She is currently dancing at this club tonight."

He shakes his head and responds, "I don't know anyone by that name, but there is a new girl. She just started a few weeks ago. Came highly recommended from L.A. I think that is the name she put on her paperwork, but you know how the girls don't use their real names around here. Highest earner. Good girl. Doesn't cause trouble. No drugs and doesn't fuck the customers. She goes by Dulce. She's a fan favorite of both guys and...girls."

That last part has my lip curling into a snarl. I adjust my diamond Cuban Link gold chain around my neck, trying to calm myself down from pushing my way into his club and snatching Alina out of there.

But I don't him to warn her that I'm here. Not yet.

"Let me see if it's her, and if it is, I want a private room with her. I don't give a shit what it costs."

"Alright, but I have to warn you. If Dulce is Alina, she doesn't dance privately."

A wave of relief washes over me because that was one of the things that had me going out of my mind, wanting to kill anyone who touches her.

"If it's her, the room, Tomas. Don't make me ask twice."

"Fine, have a look and signal my guy. I'll get her to go to the room, but I can't promise you she'll be nice."

He pulls the cord to let us through, but I pause and turn my head before disappearing under the curtain. "Make sure you and your goons don't hurt her or leave marks on her skin. If you do, I'll break every bone in your body and send the pieces of your body parts to your family, *entiendes*?"

His eyes widen at my threat.

"If it's her, you have my word. I won't touch her, Alex. I don't want problems with the cartel."

"Good. It would be a shame for my guys to find another spot to celebrate and hang out."

Six

ALEX

A s the curtain drops behind me, the pungent odor of smoke and cheap perfume fills the air. Heads turn as we pass the tables. The East Hillside Kings are well known to the local populace. The ink travels on our bodies like a message, the crowns painted on our necks, the khakis, and the brand-new Cortez on our feet.

The pounding beat of "Princess Diana" by Nicki Minaj and Ice Spice thumps through the speakers. As the music ramps up, my focus shifts to the stage where piles of cash are tossed like confetti.

My eyes are glued on Alina as she twirls on the pole in the middle of the stage, wearing nothing but the sticky things covering her nipples, a thong, and platform heels.

Various emotions take over me. I'm captivated, angry, aroused, jealous, and possessive of her.

When her feet touch the polished stage and she grasps the silver pole, my poor cock weeps inside my boxers, reminding me how she felt the first time I was inside her at seventeen. Perfect.

Her body is curvaceous now in all the right places I want to lick and feel. Alina is smoking hot. If you were a horny teenager, she's the girl you hang a poster of on your wall and jerk off to it.

When I noticed how she was staring intently at something, my eyes narrowed, and I followed her gaze to find out where. Another wave of red-hot jealousy crests over me. It's aimed right at Julio as he stares at her just like the rest.

I can't blame him, but I hate myself for feeling this way when I shouldn't. Every time I look at her, all the feelings I locked away when I was seventeen surfaces, and then the guilt for going behind my friend's back telling me I was wrong for wanting her tries to take over but it doesn't win this time and I think it never did.

The need to get her away from prying eyes has me nodding to Tomas's security, indicating that I have found who I'm looking for.

Carlito approaches me before I make my way to the back of the club.

He leans in to say, "Damn, *ese*. I hate to tell you this, but you're well over your head. With all due respect, carnal. She's... Look at the crowd. She has all the *vatos* going crazy."

It's a struggle to hold myself back from going up there and cart her ass off stage by her luscious hair. She may have gotten away with dancing in L.A. under her brother's watch, but I'm different.

"You're not helping, ese. I'm trying not to make a scene," I growl.

As soon as the words roll off my tongue, a stupid motherfucker steps up with a wad of cash, eyeing Alina like she's the only one in the room. He waits to be allowed to put the money on the string of the thong tied at her hips, and my stomach sinks. My heart constricts at the expression that crosses her face, telling me this is the part she *hates.*

Why, baby?

She's too smart for this, and it kills me to know that she has had to expose herself to this life when she has a brother who can take care of her. We make enough to support our families.

Seven

ALINA

The other Kings lurking behind Julio causes my heart to pound. I chew on my lip because they found me, and I try not to wince at the lustful look that Julio aims at me.

The thought of Danny comes to mind thinking he found me and Julio was sent to warn me, but Danny hasn't contacted me, and he also wouldn't be standing around watching me work. He'd corner me until I spread my legs and hit me when I didn't give his desired response.

As Tomas's head of security approaches, I quickly pull on the robe.

"Someone is asking for you, Dulce. "He waves his hand toward the hallway."Please follow me."

Bewildered, I ask, "Who and why?"

He shrugs. "Tomas didn't give me specifics. He requested to escort you to the back room."

I've reinstated multiple times that I don't provide private dances.

"It could be Jared Leto requesting me to give him a private anything, and my answer will still be no. No money in the world will get me to do it. No exceptions, Alan."

I just can't bring myself to do it. I already have one monster I'm running from I don't need another one taking interest.

A sly grin upturns his lips like it's no big deal. "In my opinion, that is not the case. If it helps, I'll wait outside the door. You can walk in, and if anything seems off, just leave."

Thankfully, Alan is not a creep who tries to fondle the dancers hoping to get lucky. He watches out for us and makes sure no one gets too handsy and crosses the line.

I nod, crossing my arms over my waist defensively and follow him to the back room.

We reach a pink door that leads to a private room. The corridor is lit only by a neon pink, and there are black lights over the cheap posters of naked girls on the walls, reminding me of what goes on back here.

I lick my lips nervously. My hands tremble because it could be anyone inside that room with the right influence or money.

When Alan turns the knob, I shut my eyes.

My eyes flutter open when there's a change in the air—charged with energy. After a few seconds, Alan nudges his head for me to go inside when I don't move.

When I walk in, the last person sitting in the wide black chair is staring at me with a pissed-off expression. Alex.

I nod at Alan, and he shuts the door. I take a second to admire the devastatingly attractive man who has stolen my heart despite everything. He has that bad boy look with all his ink and a tiny diamond nose piercing. Adorned in a simple white t-shirt, contrasting the swirls of beautiful ink, tells you a story like a book you don't want to close until you turn the last page.

I wished I could have been a part of his story, but unfortunately, not all girls are lucky, and some of us wind up here instead of living a fairy tale. I have the scars in my heart and skin to prove it. It's better to be angry than accept the reality about Alex. I'm the one who could never get the guy, but that's okay. I've been blessed with someone more important.

"What do you want?" I ask.

His finger beckons me, and I tighten my arms over my body, ensuring the robe covers me like a suit of armor, preventing him from seeing what he already saw while I was on stage. I'm ashamed that he saw me, but this is how I've provided for my son and paid for college. Cliché as it may be, I don't give a fuck at what he thinks of me right now.

"Are you trying to piss me off, Princessa?" His gaze gently climbs from my platform shoes to my eyes as he questions me.

I've never heard him call me that before and I need to stop trying to make it bigger than it is. Undoubtedly, he uses the same name for the harem of women he sleeps with.

I recall the day at the wedding when he called Luciana "*Preciosa*," which means beautiful in Spanish, and the initial excitement fizzles out like a match with too little fire.

"I don't see how that is possible when I didn't ask you to come here. I never mentioned where I worked, and frankly, it's none of your business. I know you had me followed."

He chuckles while scratching the cross tattoo beneath his eye and cocking his head. He removes a handgun from his waistband and places it on the black table next to the chair where a tray of condoms sits, prompting me to wonder how he was allowed inside with it until I remembered that he's a King.

A cartel king.

The sight of the gun doesn't faze me, though.

"It doesn't change that you think working here will fly with me. I've seen you and...had you. I promise, Alina, that I will not hurt you. You don't have to be shy with me, baby, when you were practically swinging on a pole outside, naked."

My rational self tells me he should call me Alina, but the rest of his words fan the flames of my hatred for him like the phantom tongues of an oxygen-starved fire.

I curl my lip.

"I'm not your *Princessa*, for starters. To you, I am nothing more than my brother's favor. Stop wasting my time with your questions and bullshit."

"Pack your shit. I'm taking you home," he says sternly.

An amused laugh bursts free, and I roll my eyes. "Wow, *cabron*. Do you really believe you can simply walk in here, snap your fingers, and I'll run out of here?" I move forward till my eyes are level with his without flinching. My chest heaves at the intensity of my rage. "*No mames*. Go home and fuck the bitches hanging around like stray cats." He blinks. "Andale, you still have time. I get off in two hours and will be back with Maxim. Just make sure you tell the next *pendeja* to keep it down because a *pinche cabron* like you just thinks about yourself while trying to get your nut off--when a little boy is trying to sleep in the next room." He recoils like I slapped him, but it's the truth. I continue, "He hates falling asleep with his headphones on."

Alex is like an endless source of frustration. The first two weeks we stayed at his house, he had a woman in the next room, and I had to listen to them while my insides caved in.

Like always, he doesn't apologize and changes the subject.

"How long have you been doing this, Alina?"

I scoff. "What. You're going to save me? Tell me I could do better, huh?"

He pins me with a heated stare.

"Eighteen."

He rests his arms on his knees and asks,"How much do you need, Alina?"

I turn away and sigh. "Go home, Smiley."

He charges and pushes me against the door, grasping my arm and pinning me with the length of his body.

"Get your shit. You no longer work here, and I swear to God, Alina, if I ever find you dancing naked anywhere, I will toss you over my knee and punish you, *entiendes*?"

His nose rubs against the skin of my neck, making me dizzy with want. His eyes trail the length of my body until his lips are inches from mine. I nod. "Good. Now, get your shit."

I press my hands against his chest pushing him away and leave the room.

Eight

ALINA

As much as I want to rebel, I have to see if I can at least work as a waitress instead. It's a lot less money and more hours, but I have to make money. Knowing Alex, he will make sure I don't work at all, and the last thing I need is to be dependent on him for anything.

My footsteps slow when I spot a sleek black Plymouth parked next to my Camry. Alex leans on the side of his car. I head over, acting like there isn't nine gang members, including Carlito and Julio, aren't waiting for me.

A cloud of smoke swirls in the air in front of me, and I scrunch my nose at the smell of marijuana. I hate drugs, avoid drinking, and definitely don't smoke.

"Throw it out," Alex says to one of the guys.

"For real, *ese*? Damn."

"If he didn't make you come here and spy on me like a bunch of snitches, you'd be smoking that in peace right now," I say.

"Do I have to tell the snitches to drive your car to make sure you pick up Maxim and head straight home?" Alex asks in a mocking tone.

"Get fucked."

Alex smiles. "I'm sure your fans would love that," he says, his voice dripping with sarcasm.

Julio sucks his teeth.

His eyes dart to Julio. "You got a problem, *cabron*? Because she doesn't understand the danger she is putting herself in on top of that piece of shit looking for her after he left her on the kitchen floor for her son to find."

I step forward, getting in Alex's face. "Oh, I'm stupid now for working here? You're going to talk about me to everyone like I'm some dumb *pendeja*. Well, newsflash. I dance, not fuck, and if Joker wanted me dead, I would be."

He clenches his jaw. "When your brother saw you at the hospital, you didn't look too hot and your son was crying. I'd say you were almost there, so why don't you put that bitchy attitude you have and aim it elsewhere and think for a second, Alina, that I'm not your enemy, and if it was up to me, you wouldn't be dancing for a buck and you sure as hell wouldn't be here."

I blink, feeling the sting of tears, but brush it off because of course he doesn't want me here or in any part of his life.

"Carlito, drive Alina's car and meet me at the house. I'll take her to go pick up Maxim at Hector's." Alex holds the passenger door open looking at me and demands, "Give me the keys."

I hand him the keys, but then voices travel from the exit of the club toward the back parking lot. "Damn, baby. If you needed a ride, I could have given you one." It's the same guy that tipped me three hundred dollars on stage. Alan usually walks me out discreetly to my car, making sure no one is let out until I drive off.

"I'm good, thanks," I reply.

"Are you sure? I could give you a really good ride for the right price."

Fuck, does he not see who the hell is with me? I'm surrounded by gangbangers.

Alex slides the gun from his waist and walks over to the guy.

My heart begins to pound erratically. Holy shit. Alex aims the gun right at the man and shoots him in the balls. He drops to his knees, and the other men try to flee but are intercepted by the Kings.

Julio covers the man's mouth to stifle his sobs while Alex lowers his gun to point it between his eyes.

"The first mistake was putting your hands on her. The second mistake"--BANG--"was thinking she was a whore." The man slumps forward with his eyes wide open.

My hands tremble uncontrollably. Alex just...killed him like it was nothing.

He turns and nods to one of the Kings standing behind the trunk of his car. "Clean it up," he orders, then looks at me. "Get in the car, Alina."

I slide inside his car without a fight. Because for the first time, I'm scared of Alex. Gone is the seventeen-year-old bad boy I fell for, and in his place, is a ruthless monster.

Nine

ALINA

I tuck a sleeping Maxim in the bed and make my way to the shower. I've had a long night and can't get over what Alex did to that guy back at the club. I know he deserved to get his ass kicked, but instead, someone got killed and it was because of me.

After rinsing off, I slide the glass door open and freeze.

"What the hell are you doing in here?" I whisper-yell, trying to cover my naked body with my hands.

Alex cocks head to the side. "I came in to get a closer look."

"Get out."

He walks closer and pushes my hands aways from my breasts. "I don't remember seeing these so big when we were younger."

I roll my eyes, placing my hands back on my breasts, trying to hide them from his gaze looking over for my towel. "Get out, Smiley."

His eyes are hard and pitch black under the white light of the bathroom. His expression is scrutinizing and mocking, but at the same time, there is a sense of disappointment. The look in his eyes as it travels over my body is not of a man that finds a woman attractive while she is standing naked and wet from a shower. Maybe he finds me disgusting and unattractive because I'm certainly not the same girl when I was seventeen.

Stretch marks cover my thighs and lower stomach. My hips are wider and my butt is fuller. I'm not his type compared to the skinnier women I have seen him with. Like the one who left his room on the second day I was here, or Luciana, the woman he fell in love with . They are all petite, beautiful, and skinny. I'm none of those things.

"Funny, you have no problem twirling naked on a pole in a club full of strangers, but I walk in and you're suddenly shy? It's not like no one has seen your body. There isn't much left to figure out anyway."

My heart sinks. He must think I'm proud of being a stripper. I didn't have a choice. But I'll never explain that to him because he doesn't deserve to know the truth.

Hating him even more for making me feel like I'm worthless, I reach out so I can grip the end of the towel on the hook behind him on the wall, not giving a shit if I wet him. Fuck him. I drape myself and glare at him.

"Then I can continue working there. Like you said, there's nothing left to figure out. You're no different from any other man in my life."

I try to side-step him, and he moves. Just as I'm about to open the door, he pushes me up against the door. He wraps his hand around my throat so I have no choice but to look up at him.

"You were never like this, Alina. I know that asshole did a number on you, but your brother would have helped you if you let him. All you had to do is tell him what was going on and he would have stepped in. You don't have to strip in a club." If only he knew. "I can't tell you what to do because we both know you're going to do it behind my back, but I mean well. It's not safe. If you need money––"

My jaw hardens. "I don't want your money or your pity. I already told you. I'm here because of my brother, and I'm doing this for my son." I swallow when his hand falls. "Now, I need to get some sleep. So that tomorrow night, I can get a head start in showing everyone what I look like without my clothes."

"Alina–"

I open the door and practically sprint to the spare room, careful to not wake Maxim as I shut the door behind me. Teary-eyed, I take in my son, asleep on the bed, trying to sooth my nerves.

But I can't. As much as I try, the tears fall.

Alex said more than I wished to hear. And the worst part is, I let it get to me.

Ten

ALINA

I pour the pancake batter on the pan, watching the bubbles form on top. Maxim and I are heading to his surprise. I made enough money last night even though someone's life paid the price. I tell myself I can't think about that right now or what the Kings did to cover it up. It's not like my brother hadn't done the same back in L.A. I did my best keeping Maxim away as much as possible so he would never see his uncle's wrongdoings.

"Are you sure you can't tell me, Mama?"

"You will see when we get there," I respond, turning slightly.

Maxim is swinging his legs while seated at the table, waiting for his pancakes. I wonder where he stores all the food. He is slim, with a tan complexion and black straight hair like mine. He's my little ball of energy.

"Can you give me a hint?"

I crinkle my nose at him. "Nope. Nice try though."

He picks up his fork and begins to tap it on the table. "Is it a toy?"

"Nope. Put the fork down, Maxim." He places the fork down and lets out an audible sigh.

His brown eyes find mine; his forehead crinkling, and I know it's because he just remembered something. "Did he find us, Mom?"

I avert my gaze and slide the pancake off the pan on top of the pile on the plate. "No, he hasn't found us. We're safe here."

He is talking about Danny, and as much as I hid what Danny did to me, I know Maxim isn't stupid to not know about the bruises. When Maxim called his uncle, I knew that no matter what Danny did or threatened me with, I couldn't put Maxim through that again.

The front door opens, Julio, Hector, and Carlito walk in with a few other Kings trailing behind them.

"What's up, *chavalito*?" Julio greets Maxim.

"Hi," Maxim says but stops swinging his legs. The beaming smile he had and the light in his eyes are gone. I guess he's shy.

I wave at the other guys who pass by, giving me head nods.

Julio steps into the kitchen and smiles. "Hey, Alina." His eyes look at the plate while I turn the burner off. "Pancakes, huh?"

"Yeah, do you want some?"

"If there is enough for one more."

I set the plate on the table. "Of course there is. Have a seat."

But he keeps standing in the middle of the kitchen. Waiting.

I serve Maxim and then Julio.

The door opens and closes in the hallway, and based on the murmurs and the sudden shift of energy around me, I know it's Alex.

When he walks in the kitchen, I notice two things. Both Maxim and Alex are scowling. Alex looks at Julio, and without another word, plops himself in the seat and picks up the syrup. You have got to be kidding me. Seriously?

"Thank you for the breakfast, Alina," Alex says in an even tone.

"That wasn't for you," I snap.

Alex begins to cut his pancakes like he is ignoring what I just said. "It is now," he says with a triumphant smirk.

I roll my eyes and turn to get another plate, but Julio steps in front of me. "It's okay, *Princessa*. Eat before the food gets cold. I'm good."

"Why didn't you sit at the table?"

Julio swallows and gives me a side grin. "I was waiting for you to sit down first so I can hold your chair." A fork clanks on a plate, and Julio looks nervously behind me.

I walk toward the chair, hoping to prevent this situation from escalating. I know Alex is holding back because of Maxim.

Julio moves to hold the chair out for me. I try to not get choked up because no man has ever done this before for me.

"I'm sorry. I didn't know that was the reason. It's the first time. Thank you."

"You're welcome," Julio says before walking away.

"First time for what?" Alex asks.

My eyes meet his hard ones, and I lick my lips, grabbing the bottle of syrup. "First time someone waited for me to sit down or hold my chair."

I place the bottle on the table and turn to Maxim to make sure he isn't making a mess. I caress his cheek, but he tosses me a sad smile.

"Todo bien?" Is everything okay? I ask Maxim.

He nods.

"Do you want to feed the fish with me after we eat, Maxim?" Alex asks.

Maxim stiffens and replies, "No, that's okay. You can have him. I don't want him anymore."

My eyebrows pull into a frown wondering what's wrong with him.

"How come? I thought you loved the fish and we promised we would feed it together every morning?"

Maxim looks at me, ignoring Alex. "Can I call tio Joaquin? I need to talk to him?"

I tilt my head in curiosity. "Why? You spoke to him the day before yesterday."

Maxim pushes his plate away and gives me a hug. His next words are shocking me. "I promised him I would call him if I heard you crying." He looks up, and I try to mask the guilt off my face. "Can we call him on the way to my surprise now?"

I didn't think he heard me last night, but him questioning me about Danny and his sudden change in demeanor toward Alex make sense.

I give Maxim a tight hug to assure him I'm okay, but I make a point not to look in Alex's direction because I won't lie to Maxim. It is bad enough I have kept things from him because I have no other option. The only thing I can do is assure him that I'm fine. That we are fine.

"Yeah, go get washed up. It's okay, Maxim. Mommy gets sad sometimes."

Eleven

ALEX

Watching her get up and leave the kitchen with Maxim gutted me. What was I thinking coming at her like that after I killed that *puto* last night, only to make her feel worse about her situation by judging her for taking care of her son the only way she knows how. The fact that she was crying because of me is like rubbing salt in a gaping wound.

Hector walks into the kitchen and sits in the chair Alina just vacated. "I'm no relationship expert, *ese*. I'm probably the last person to talk about how you should treat a woman, but that woman with her little boy has been through some real fucked up shit. Whatever you did or said, fix it. She doesn't deserve anyone's judgment because Alina hasn't asked any of us for shit and has been on her own. As for that little boy, he is tired of seeing every man in her life shit on her."

I slouch in my chair, feeling like a total asshole. "I know, carnal. I fucked up. I told her shit I wasn't supposed to, but I was angry."

"Angry or jealous?"

"I don't know. All I know is that I didn't like what I saw when I went inside that club and it made me snap."

He snickers. "Like putting a bullet in that *vato's* skull when he disrespected her?"

Techincally balls and skull.

I hang my head. "Yeah, like that. I don't know, but I can't let her work there and I know she is going to do the exact opposite of what I tell her. It is not safe for her and she is hellbent on being independent."

"Then hire her to do something."

"She dances with a thong dumbass for money."

"Did you like what you saw when you saw her in there?"

I snort. "Who didn't, *cabron*. She's gorgeous."

"Does it matter who she dances for, then?"

"Yes, it does. There are *pinche cabrones* that don't keep their hands to themselves. Some idiots could stalk her, and let's not forget Joker. It's only a matter of time before he finds out where they are hiding. Then what?"

"Protect her, *cabron*. Why doesn't she dance for you?"

"Are you fucking crazy?"

"No, *pero sabes que*? I do know a club owner that entertains shit like that. Members only."

He means Leo. I grip the fork, twirling the cold piece of pancake drowning in syrup. First thing, I need to fix things with Maxim and then convince Alina not to go back to work at the Satin Doll.

"I'll figure something out. Where did she go?"

Hector pulls up his phone and sends a text. "Smokey followed her." A ding alerting a message comes through. "She's at the pet store."

"I'll be right back. Call the cleaning lady to come and clear out this mess. I don't want Alina cleaning."

"*Si, patron.*"

Twelve

ALINA

"How about one of these?" I point to the tank with similar fish. Maxim can't take his eyes off the fish that resembles the ones in Alex's house.

"How about these? They glow. I'm sure it would look really nice at the house." I close my eyes and then open them. My heart beating like a drum in my chest. I look over. Alex.

Goosebumps run down the length of my arms every time he is near. I straighten from bending to look at the fish.

He is looking at the neon freshwater fish that look like they are in a movie set of Avatar. They look awesome under the lights, but I would have to spend more than I budgeted for just a fish tank and one or two fish.

A store associate walks up, so I ask, "How much is the glo-fish setup over there?"

Maxim walks over to me with a hopeful expression.

The young guy looks at the medium-sized tank. "It would be about six hundred bucks." Shit. Okay, I guess I will have to work extra for the next three nights. I am about to tell him I'll take it until he adds, "That doesn't include the fish though." I swallow, calculating in my head.

"We'll take it, and let the little man pick out as many fish as you can put in there," Alex says, walking up.

The young guy raises his brows in surprise. "All twenty fish and the tank?" Maxim looks up at me with wide eyes, silently asking for permission to pick out the fish.

Alex moves up beside me and whispers, "It's on me, *mi reina.*" He's never called me his queen before and it rolls over my me like a caress. "*Perdoname?*"

Alex Cortez is apologizing in that sexy way of his, and I don't know what to do about it. "Let me make it right? I didn't mean to offend you, and I was wrong. I promise I'll try harder. Let me do this for him and...for you."

I nod to Maxim when the sales associate waits with the fish net near the glo-fish tank. I can't refuse in letting him get Maxim the fish, but I won't stand for Alex to hurt me again. "Don't do it again."

He caresses my cheek. "I promise, but we need to talk alone."

"He jumped out!" Maxim squeals, pointing at the net just above the water.

"It happens," the young guy says.

"I want that one." Maxim looks up at the guy. "Can you get him?"

Alex chuckles beside me and calls out, "Yo." Ben, the salesman, looks up. "You gotta a bigger tank?"

"Yeah."

"I want it and all those fish inside that tank."

Maxim looks up at Alex. "All of them?"

Alex nods. "We're friends, remember? I said sorry to your mommy, and I'm sorry."

"Alex." He slides his hand around my waist, pulling me close, and I swear I want to jump inside the tank with the fish to cool down the heat pooling between my thighs.

"Let me spoil him," he whispers.

Maxim has never been spoiled like this. Sure, I have bought him nice things, depending on how my nights went dancing but nothing like this.

"Fine, just this once."

He squeezes my waist and lowers his lips to my ear, and in a soft voice, says, "I forgot to tell you, I love your pancakes. I'm sorry I acted like an ass."

Thirteen

ALEX

My phone rings while I'm driving to the house with all the big fish tank in the back of my Mercedes G-Wagon. Joaquin. Fuck.

"Hey," I answer through the Bluetooth.

"What the fuck, *ese*?" I blink hard and wince.

"I'm guessing Alina called you."

"Yes, Alina called me, Smiley. Why is my nephew telling me he thinks you were the one to make his mother cry. I trusted you to take care of her until we catch that *puto* Joker. I know she can be a pain in the ass when someone offers her help, but that is the way she is, Smiley. I...don't blame her. She's been through a lot since our mother—"

He's pissed, I get it. If it were Linda, I would be on a warpath myself. "I know, carnal. I was mad because I found out where she worked and it pissed me off what she was doing."

"Let me guess—a strip club."

"I'm surprised you know and haven't done shit about it. *No manches, cabron.* She can't be doing that shit for money. There are animals out there and that shit is not good for Maxim."

"You think I haven't had this conversation with her? You think I" haven't tried? Fuck, Smiley. I would do anything for them. They're my family."

"Look, that is why she got upset because I was trying the same way you have, but I had to back off. The problem is, I have to convince her some other way so she can feel independent but safe too."

"What do you have in mind?"

"I'm going to talk to Leo and we'll come up with something. I gotta go. I have a fish tank to set up."

"I heard about the fish. I'm not going to ask how you convinced her to get Maxim anything, but I want to tell you something no one knows. This stays between us, carnal."

"I'm listening."

"Alina almost didn't make it during birth. I was too young to understand, let alone do anything about it, but our mother used while being pregnant with Alina. Crack and marijuana mostly. Alina was addicted to crack when she was born. We were held in child services until our mother got clean enough to get her back, but it didn't stop there. When I was gone and they were alone, she would make Alina watch her fuck so when she was older, she would know what to do to make money."

"The fuck?"

"I know, carnal. I didn't know but the damage was done. Alina didn't follow our mother's footsteps, though."

That is why she is so protective over Maxim. She trusted one guy and he fucked her over. She was taught to sell her body for a buck.

"She turned out pretty good actually. Yes, she dances but from what I have heard, no private dances. And she doesn't screw guys for money and doesn't drink or do drugs. You know the drugs and drinking part since I told you, but not the other stuff. Go easy on her, *ese*. Keep her safe and let me know if you need me to send you money for her or Maxim."

"I got it. I don't need your money, carnal. I said I'll watch her and protect her. I'll call you after I speak to Leo and tell you what I have in mind."

"Alright, gotta go... Hey, Smiley?"

"*Si, hermano?*"

"Did you really smoke that fool at the club for disrespecting my sister?"

I swallow because we both know what that means. It means I care more than I should, like she belongs to me. The same way a man responds when he needs to defend his woman's honor. It might mean an act of violence for some, but in our world, risking your life and freedom in order to take another person's life means more than anything. It means Alina is mine. I drew the line even if I won't acknowledge it, but Joaquin does. And the silence between us says everything. He knows she means more to me than I let on.

I hang up and dial Leo.

"What's up?"

"Hey. You busy?"

"Nah, but I know why you're calling, *cabron*. When is the wedding?"

"Very funny, asshole. You have a minute?"

"Yep."

"I need you to do something for me."

"Name it, *carnal.*"

Fourteen

ALINA

I walk back outside from the house while Alex and an excited Maxim set up the gigantic fish tank he bought with the rest of the Kings. My car was making a funny noise when I pulled in.

I open the driver side door and turn on the seven-year-old Toyota Camry and wince when I hear a terrible knocking sound coming from the engine when I turn the key. Shit. I bought it used and I thought this make and model would last me. I have done all the maintenance required on it to make sure I don't get stranded somewhere with Maxim.

I slam my hand on the steering wheel frustratingly and open the car door to get out, leaning down to pop the hood.

I hear the sound of footsteps behind me, but I ignore it, trying to see if I can figure this out or to see what my options are.

"What's wrong with it?" Julio asks, looking at the engine.

I shrug my shoulders. "I have no idea. It's making a noise."

"Hmm. The thing is, *Princessa*, I don't hear anything."

I turn my head and look at the big grin on his face. "Are you being funny?"

His lip curls into a smile. "I'm just sayin'. You said it was making a noise, but I don't hear anything."

"That's because the car is turned off. Wait–"

He bursts into laughter. "I know that, *carnalita*. I'm messing with you. Go turn the car on and I'll stay right here so we can hear the noise."

I roll my eyes dramatically. "Ha-ha."

I go to turn the car and wince when it makes the same noise I heard earlier when I turn the key.

"Stop!" Julio yells, and I immediately turn the car off.

"What is it?" I ask, sliding out to stand beside him. "Hey. Why are you closing it?"

"It's the starter. It needs to be replaced. Pretty soon, the car won't start."

I slam the driver's side door closed and cross my arms over my chest. "How do you know that from just hearing it?"

"Are you always this difficult when someone tries to help you out?"

"Telling me what's wrong with it is not fixing it, and that is if what you said is even right."

He tilts his head. "You think I'm wrong?"

"There is no way you can tell by just listening to me turn it on that it's the starter."

His eyes gleam as he studies me.

He smiles like he is trying to hold the laugh that wants to bubble out of his mouth. "Are you always this stubborn?"

I raise an eyebrow in challenge. "Are you always this cocky?"

"When it comes to cars, yeah." He pushes off my car and closes in. "When it comes to you, I don't know where to even start or what to say. You make me feel––star struck and...there is nothing about you I don't like."

A chill runs down my spine. I've been hit on before but none of the guys have ever said something like that.

I lick my lips nervously and say, "Look, you seem like a nice guy, but I'm not like the *hynas* that come around here. I don't screw around. Especially with members of the Kings. I think I learned my lesson. So, save yourself the trouble. You don't have to say things like that, hoping I'll sleep with you because I won't."

"But I already knew that. Bring the car by my shop in the morning to get it fixed."

I pinch my brows. "Your shop?"

"I'm a mechanic, and I have my own shop."

"Oh. I'm sorry, but how much?"

"Don't worry about that."

I let out an audible sigh. "I'm sure you don't work for free and I just can't let you fix my car without paying you. So, how much?"

"Fine, I'll fix your car if you promise to let me pick you up Friday night for dinner."

I tilt my head up and laugh. "You're better off charging me. My brother will murder you for even trying to kick it with me."

His expression is blank. I look at the front door of the house and then at him. He is staring at me and I don't know how I feel about that.

"I better get—"

He interrupts me, "I'm sorry. I–You laughed."

Smokey walks out of the house and heads over to us. He always smells like marijuana, hence how he got his name. " What do you think you're doing, *ese?* If Smiley catches you out here with Alina, he's going to kick your ass over the border into Mexico."

Julio slides his hands inside his khaki shorts. "Relax, *holmes.* I was helping her out with her car. The starter is fucked."

Smokey looks at him and his eyes land on me. "This *vato* giving you trouble?" he teases and then looks back at Julio shaking his head. "Let it go, *holmes.*"

"I don't know what you're talking about," Julio says in his defense.

Smokey points at Julio's face and his eyes narrow. "She's Joaquin's sister, *cabron.* Keep it in your pants or it'll get chopped off."

At least I'm not the only one warning poor Julio.

"Let me know how much it will cost. I have to head back inside," I tell him and walk away.

When I'm halfway down the concrete path, I hear Julio tell

Smokey. "What the fuck, *ese*. I really like her and I was trying to talk to her until you showed up and fucked it up for me. I got her to laugh."

Smokey chuckles. "You're a fool. You can buy that woman a new car and she will still turn you down, *ese*. That is before her brother and Smiley kill you for trying."

Fifteen

ALINA

I walk into the living room after getting ready to head to work. Some of the guys are watching a boxing match on TV. Alex is still getting the fish tank cycled. It is beautiful. All the fish swimming in their vibrant colors. The sound of the water from the filter gives off a calming effect to the space. It's nice. Like a real home. A home I didn't have growing up, unless it was filled with gang members and girls, hoping to get lucky with one of them.

"Hey Alex, I need to get work? I'm having trouble with my car. Can drop me off? I can take an Uber back."

Alex closes the door of the new cabinet he purchased for the fish, not acknowledging me at all. My eyes dart around the room but the guys don't say anything.

"Alex," I call out.

"I'll take you," he says softly and finally looks up. "You're dancing?"

My heart is beating inside my chest.

"Yeah, it's kinda the point."

He points at my feet. "In those?"

I look at my sandals. I have a pound of makeup on, but I'm wear something comfortable. I don't want to walk around wearing something a stripper would normally wear.

I snort and hold up my duffle bag. "They're in here. If you're interested, you can borrow them when I'm done using them tonight."

Alex cocks his head, his eyes challenging me to push, stepping closer until we are inches apart. "I think we both know who they look better on, *muneca*." He lowers his voice. "Be careful Alina, I might want to watch."

My nostrils flare, and I step closer. He wants to play games. My chest almost touches his now. I swipe my finger over the skin on his throat with the crown tattoo of the Kings. He swallows when I purr, "You want to watch me, Smiley? Aren't you afraid you're violating some bro code with my brother?"

I'm pushing him because we both know he wouldn't touch me in front of the other Kings. It would mean that we have something going on.

"Everyone here knows that is untrue. The same way they know you dance basically naked in front of strangers. Stop playing games and let's get you to work."

He walks toward the front door, holding it open, and waves his hand so I can walk out. "Come on, your customers are waiting."

I bite the inside of my cheek to keep myself from lashing out. The taste of blood on my tongue is a welcome experience to match the way my blood boils in my veins. I lower my gaze, avoiding the looks of pity on the guys' faces.

"See you tomorrow, Alina," Julio says, but I don't respond because I have learned that pride is the rope that keeps you from falling in a well of tears.

I walk over to Alex's Plymouth. The same one he picked me up from the Satin Doll.

"Where are you going?" He asks walking in another direction.

"Hurry up, you're making me late. My customers are going to complain."

He walks over to his Mercedes G-wagon and opens the passenger door. "Get in, Alina."

I sigh, wondering why he wants to drive me in his fancy car.

When I sit still inside dropping my bag on my feet, He leans in and grips the seatbelt over buckling me in. The heat and scent of his skin inches away from my face but I avert my eyes looking out the driver's side window refusing to let him get to me.

When I hear the click of the seatbelt, I face forward and his dark eyes are fixated on mine. "You love to test me, Alina. You're playing a dangerous game with me."

"Then watch what you say to me. I'm not one of your *pinche pendejas* you can talk to however you want."

His jaw hardens and his eyes turn cold when he says, "Or what? You're threatening me? With what? The fact you begged me to pop your cherry when we were seventeen and tell your brother on me?" I slide my hand down slowly and click on the seat belt, holding it in my hand, waiting until he pulls away so I can get out. "You think because of that, you're going to manipulate me? I'm trying to help you and keep you safe. That *pinche* rat out there looking for you. You think by challenging me in front of the others will get whatever reaction you want out of me. What do you want from me, Alina?"

"I want you to get out of my face. I hate you," I spit.

He closes his eyes and pulls away, closing the door.

I let go of the seatbelt and grab my bag, waiting until he slides in the car, and once the door closes, I open mine and run toward my car.

"Alina!" Alex shouts, followed by a slew of curses.

I slide the key in the ignition, hoping the car turns on. When it does, I pull out. The adrenaline coursing through my veins gives me the courage to do what I've always known how to do. Run.

I drive until I'm at a shopping center, making sure I'm not being followed. I park the car and get out at a small restaurant.

I place an order and sit.

My hands are shaking so I place them down on my lap when the waitress brings my order. I look at the sandwich for a second, trying to calm myself down.

"I figured you would be happy that you got away from me." I

look up and rapidly blink, hoping that this is a dream. Danny is facing me in the booth, wearing a gray hoodie. The joker he tattooed over the Kings' signature crown tattoo on his neck with its evil smile mocks me like this is a joke. "Why are you crying? Aren't you happy to see me, *Preciosa*? It's been a while."

"Leave me alone, Joker."

I stopped calling him Danny long ago. He lied to me. I feel like I've been sentenced to life in an imaginary prison.

"Aww, is that any way to greet me?" He taps the table with his gold ring on his pinky finger. His dark eyes are cold and calculating. "How's my little boy?"

"We have an agreement, and Maxim is not part of it. Stop playing games."

He nods and leans back. "Go back to L.A."

"I can't. My brother sent us here and I had to give up my apartment. They're looking for you for what you did to me."

"That wouldn't have happened if you would stop crying when I fucked you. A man doesn't like to have the woman he is fucking crying while he's trying to get his nut off."

Asshole.

"What do you want?"

"What I have always wanted. I don't have much time before Smiley gets here, but this is your only warning. His time will come. He wants to play the gangster. But what he doesn't get is that I'm the one in control. He thinks he is untouchable because of who his mother spread her legs for, but in reality, he is weak."

"You need to stop, Joker. The Kings don't play games. There is no point in what you are doing. It solves nothing."

"It does for me," he grits through clenched teeth. "It should have been me they sent here to lead the Kings but he wanted to prove that he was better than me. This was all before he found out who his father was. He was nothing but the bastard child of a narco. A hidden scion of the cartel that only cares about himself. Haven't I proven that?"

Danny is crazy. He has this chip on his shoulder for Alex. Ever since they made Alex the leader of the East Hillside Kings with direct connections to the cartel, making more money than all the members combined only to him find out who his father is, Danny wants to destroy him.

"You need to let it go, Joker. Let me go."

He shakes his head. "I can't do that. See, I like your cunt. I like those tits I made you get and I like to watch the way you twirl on that pole, knowing your brother and none of the Kings can do shit about it. Because we both know what's at stake, Alina. If you don't do what I say and how I say it, I'll take Maxim after I let everyone in the cartel I work with run a train on you and slit your throat so I can let another whore I fuck raise your son."

Dread pools in my stomach. Needles prick my throat because I know he would do it. He's shown me videos of what they do. He hit me because I didn't want to have sex with him many times, and when I had to, I would be crying when Maxim was asleep. I always cry silently when Danny touches me, but that night, he wanted pictures of me and I refused. I started to sob and he slapped me when I pushed him off me, telling to stop tearing at my clothes. He punched me hard and all I remember is everything going dark and me waking up at the hospital with a pissed off Joaquin barking at the nurses.

"I can't go back to L.A. I don't have money and I need my car fixed."

He snickers. "What's wrong, not making money at the Satin Doll?"

My eyes narrow because that means he knows exactly where I have been this whole time. I lied when I told Alex I hated him. If he only knew how much I hate the man sitting in front of me. He is no different than the human traffickers he works for. Danny is greedy and unhinged because of his quest for money and the need to manipulate people to get what he wants.

"Smiley doesn't like the idea of me working there?"

"Are you fucking him?"

"That goes against the rules, doesn't it?"

"Allowing a cock other than mine inside any orifice in your body is against my rules. You can show it, but no one can touch it. Break the rule and you will see what happens to you."

That is another one of his rules. No one can touch me but him. He loves the fact that he is the only one that can touch me. I'm sure he has plenty of pictures he has collected of me to boast about it. He has never showed them to me but his phone aiming at my pussy and him telling me to pose for him is proof enough. I was able to take pictures on my phone when he left his phone open and I saw them for myself. My life of hell for almost six years for choosing the wrong man. I never thought where I would end up or how what I would be doing at the age of twenty-four.

"Are you fucking him, Alina?"

"No, he isn't interested in me that way so you don't have to worry about it."

"How do you know? He isn't a monk."

"I can hear him with them or rather the women he takes to bed."

He chuckles. "Wait? He brings women while you sleep in the next room with Maxim? Don't tell me the poor boy is listening to that shit."

"He sleeps with his headphones until he falls asleep."

"And you?"

"Me what?"

I lose my appetite when he grabs the uneaten sandwich and takes a bite. "Do you listen to the girls moan while he is fucking them?"

I didn't have a choice the first time. I don't think he realized they were being too loud, but it hurt me deep inside to have to hear it. I got angry and then I went to the bathroom to cry. The next day, I acted like nothing. My mask was firmly in place even though I was dying inside. I'm used to feeling like that, unwanted and mistreated. Hell, even my mother didn't want me either. I'm sure she didn't care if I lived or died. I don't know why Joaquin sent me over here so Alex, of all people, could protect me from my fate. The only life I've lived is the time I have with Maxim.

The man currently scarfing down the sandwich I have to pay for knows that Maxim is the only reason I'm still here. He knows I'm holding on for him.

"I have learned to tune them out. You can run along and be a smuggler. I'm doing exactly what you asked. I'll keep quiet and you come and go as you please."

He places the crust of the bread down on the plate and throws money on the table. "Meet me in the bathroom before that *pendejo* shows up."

"Why?"

But I know why.

He tilts his head. "You know why. I want you to feel what they felt when he was fucking them." My eyes fill with tears. "Don't piss me off, Alina. You already know what that pain feels like."

Sixteen

ALEX

I have been driving for about an hour when I remember that she has a tracker placed in her car. When I finally find her, she is walking out of a small restaurant on the outskirts of the east of Hillside.

I'm pissed at her for leaving. It was stupid and dangerous, but it was all my fault. I pushed.

Hector has intel on Joker and he's here in Arizona. It doesn't take a genius to know what he is here for. He is running for a cartel organization that runs the human trafficking ring in and out of Mexico. The kind of organization that sells and rapes woman on the black market.

I stop my SUV next to her car, and I fire a text to Smokey to take her car back to the house. I fucked up again. I'm always fucking up when it comes to her, but she loves to push me. I can't show anyone I have a weakness when it comes to her or that we slept together. It's a risk that can cost me my relationship with Joaquin if I'm not careful. If he finds out, he will want me away from her, and I'm the only one that can protect her. I know that, and he knows it too.

I walk up to her. "Get in the car, Alina." She doesn't look up at me, and I know I'm the last person she wants to see. She looks upset, and I feel like such a dick. She rubs her hands over her arms like she is cold, and I pull my hoodie over my head. "Here," I say, handing her the black sweater.

"I don't want anything from you." The slight tremble in her voice is the only thing that tells me that she is trying not to break apart. "Can you take me to pick up Maxim, please?"

"Of course, *Preciosa*."

She chuckles sarcastically, and when her eyes meet mine, they are red, and her expression is defeated. Like she has been working three days straight with no sleep. "Don't call me that. It's better to just be civil with each other. I don't want to fight. I can leave and go back to L.A. You don't have to look at my face ever again."

"Don't say that, Alina. Look, I'm sorry. I was angry–"

She raises her hand to stop me. "I don't want to hear it, Smiley. You don't owe me shit. Whatever happened was a long time ago and it was a mistake. No one has to know. Trust me, I'll make sure of it. Come to think of it, you're right, I was desperate. I begged you and you took pity."

She doesn't deserve an asshole like me.

"Don't cry, Alina. Please." A single tear slides down her cheek, and I move to catch it with my thumb, but she steps back.

"Don't touch me. I don't want you to ever touch me."

It feels like a steel door has just slammed in my face. An impenetrable wall I can't break.

"Alina, I'm sorry. Let me make it right. "

"Can you go back in time, *cabron*? If you could do that, then everything would be right again. You can erase the night I begged you to sleep with me. Oh, you can change who I had Maxim with and get rid of Joker, but the sad truth is, you're not Superman. You're not Flash. You're just an asshole giving me shit because every time I walk in a room and you're in it, the shame haunts you."

"That's not true. I don't regret it, Alina. I'm honored that you chose me."

"That's the problem, Smiley."

"Alex. You have more of a right than almost anyone to call me Alex."

"You didn't choose me. You have never chosen me for anything and I'm okay with that. I moved on and so have you. We're practically strangers. We are no different than a one-night stand."

She walks around and gets in the car, dismissing our conversation. A car pulls up and I nod to Smokey to get her car, hoping it starts. I slide into the driver's side, feeling like I just lost something monumental. It's like a piece of me that I can't get back.

Seventeen

ALINA

I make it home in a sour-ass mood. Julio, Carlito and Smokey keep giving me worried looks when they saw Alina.

My phone keeps going off. I check it and the *hyna* that I slept with trying to forget the fact that Alina was in the next room keeps calling me because all it took was one look at Alina and I wanted to fuck her. I've been trying to battle the urge of wanting to pull Alina by her long silky hair and tie her up to my bed.

"Damn, *ese*. Who the fuck is blowing up your phone?" Smokey asks.

I take a deep breath and answer so I can break off whatever Camila thought we had. Again.

"Why aren't you answering? I texted Carlito and he said you guys are chillin' at the house. Did I do something wrong?"

"I'm busy. What do you need?"

"I was wondering if you want me to come over later. It's been a while," she purrs.

"Camila, it was a one-time thing."

"What do you mean by that?"

I roll my eyes. This is like the fourth time I tell her the same thing. I don't do repeats because they all want something more.

Something I am not able to give anyone. I don't work a nine-to-five job. What I do is dangerous and no woman should have to wait up for me, hoping I'm still alive.

"It means exactly that. One time and that is it."

"Was I that bad?" she whines.

She wants me to admit that I found her good in bed. So that she can tell everyone and boast about it. The truth is, she wasn't Alina. No one is. I haven't found a woman who looked at me the way Alina did that one night or felt the way she felt when she was in my arms.

"Camila, I'm not going to answer that. All I'm going to say is that it was a one-time thing and nothing you can do or say is going to change my mind."

"Is it because of the girl sleeping in the next room. The stripper? You're fucking her, aren't you?"

My jaw ticks and I grip my phone hard. So, I do what I do best when I'm angry. I hit where it hurts. "Yeah, it is, and I am. Call her that again and you'll be sorry, Camila."

She huffs. "But she isn't a one-time thing?"

I hang up on her. If it were up to me, Alina would be an everyday thing.

Shuffling down the hallway catches my attention. A sleepy Maxim appears, rubbing his eyes.

I bolt out of the couch and pick him up before he bumps into something.

"Hey, Maxim. What's wrong?"

"Mommy is in the shower and is taking too long. I'm thirsty and I want chocolate milk."

I carry him through the kitchen and set him down at the table and open the fridge. I grin when I see a mason jar with one prepared for him with his name and chocolate milk written across it.

I serve Maxim and tuck him back to sleep. There are only a few hours before morning so I decide to let him get some sleep and he can brush his teeth when he wakes up.

Walking back out of the room, I can hear the shower running from the hallway bathroom.

I shouldn't, but fuck it. I use the skeleton key and open the door, slipping inside. The steam of the shower almost suffocates me when I shut the door softly, flicking the lock. I pull off my sweater and t-shirt.

"Alina?"

"Leave me alone, Smiley. Get out," she croaks.

"I'm not leaving until you open the shower door and look at me."

"No."

"Fine." I open the door, and my dick twitches at the sight of her voluptuous body. Jesus. Her body is pure sin. The only thing I don't like is that she has been crying.

She moves to cover herself with her hands, but I slide my sneakers and socks off along with my pants and boxers.

"What the hell are you doing?"

"You won't come out or look at me so I'm coming in. Maxim woke up."

Her head whips toward me, and she is about to push me out of the way.

"Relax." I hold her upper arms, careful not to grip too tight. "He wanted chocolate milk and I took care of it. I put him to sleep."

Her head tilts and our eyes meet. My hands slide down her arms; the spray of the water hitting her back causing a mist of water and steam to surround us in a bubble. I close the shower door.

"Aren't you afraid what the guys will think?"

"Does it look like I care right now what they think?"

My fingers slide down her ribs to the indent of her waist, pausing right before the flare of her hip. Her skin is wet and hot from the warm water under my fingers.

I snag my bottom lip, trying to keep myself from lifting her leg over my hip and fucking her because my dick is rock hard between us. The tip of my cock hitting the flat part of her lower belly aches to sink deep inside her.

Her eyes caress my chest down to my cock with the piercing at the tip. She swallows and points at it. "That wasn't there before."

I point out at her huge breasts. I'm not into plastic surgery, but she looks like a sex doll, and my cock twitches in agreement. "Those weren't there either?"

She grins. I want to show her how gorgeous she is without words. I want her to feel it. Fuck it, I want her to know.

I step closer so that the head of my cock rubs against her skin. The sound of the shower drowns out the whimper that escapes her throat. I lean close so that my lips are near her ear. "Now I'm the one begging for you to touch me."

Her lips part, and our foreheads touch. The water cascades down our skin. The tips of her hard nipples press against my lower chest. Firm and perfect. "Touch me, Alina," I rasp.

Her fingertips tease my skin down my torso over the muscles on my stomach until she reaches my cock. Her delicate hands wrap around it, and my nostrils flare. She strokes my cock and rubs her thumb over the tip of the piercing. Fuck.

I push her against the tile, dipping my head so I can capture her lips with mine, and when our tongues meet, we groan.

We kiss as if we're in a war. A war I'm willing to fight her in. Her lips are full and her tongue is perfect. I want to feel it everywhere. I want to feel her everywhere.

My mouth nibbles and sucks her bottom lip down to her chin. Her hands stroke my cock from base to tip.

My left hand cradles her breast, and I dip my head and suck her nipple. I trail my tongue over the swell of her breast, and she lets out a small moan when my right hand on her hip slides down her inner thigh, moving to her slit. Her neck arches when I reach her clit, rubbing it like I'm creating a cadence.

Wanting her to feel more, I lift her leg over my hip. Her eyes widen, and I smirk. "Come for me," I demand, slipping two fingers inside her pussy.

It's tight and so fucking wet. She grinds her hips against my hand, and I reciprocate. I'm so fucking hard for her. I want to take her right here in the shower, but I know it's not the time. There are too many emotions between us. There are too many pieces that are not yet aligned, but I know I want to give her this. I want her to feel how she affects me.

"Spread your pussy with your other hand."

She takes two of her fingers from her other hand and does what I ask. She spreads her pink pussy so I can slide my fingers in and out. "I want you, Alina. I've always wanted you."

It's not a lie. I have wanted her. She has had my attention since we were seventeen.

"Alex," she moans softly.

She's close, and so am I. I need to get something off my chest before the moment is over because once we both come, reality will set in, and she will retreat inside her shell. Her steel wall will go back up.

"I say stupid shit because we both know I want you for myself. I know it's wrong of me because I can't be what you want me to be but you drive me crazy, Alina. I also can't let a man put his hands on you." My dick pulses in her hand because I'm about to come but I wait until her pussy clenches my fingers and I hit her G-spot, causing her release to crest, my name escaping her lips against my tongue.

I don't stop kissing her while she rides the wave of her orgasm, and she doesn't stop jerking me off. I keep her leg over my hip. "Look at my cock, baby."

She does what I ask, and when my cum shoots out, I paint it on her pussy, rubbing it with the tip of my dick down her slit marking her. When I'm done, I swipe the head of my cock and slide my fingers insider her mouth so she can taste me. "You're the only woman that I have gone bare for and the only pussy I have filled with my cum. You," I shut off the water, not letting her wash my cum of her skin.

"What are you doing? Turn it back on."

I step out of the shower and dry off. I get dressed and check my phone. Two hours until sunrise. "Don't wash my cum, and go sleep in my bed. I have a proposition for you in the morning."

"But–"

"Just do it, Alina."

Eighteen

ALINA

I tip-toe after the coast is clear and Alex has sent everyone home. I'm surprised I didn't hear any of them question him, but then I remember that Alex is the son of a notorious drug lord. He's the son of a cartel king.

A cartel king that saved me from falling apart inside the shower moments ago. It was like his soul knew something his mind didn't. When I think of letting go because it is all too much for me, he does something that pulls me back to him. He erases it what I'm trying to forget.

When I close his bedroom door behind me, I find him setting up a small TV next to his bigger one.

"I placed a small camera in the room and connected to this TV so we can watch Maxim."

The man is better than any mother, I swear. Fuck a baby monitor, Alex places a camera so I can have a peace of mind.

"Thank you."

"I'll leave it and give you access on your phone in case he's asleep and you're in the kitchen or something. Now that I know he wakes up in the middle of the night because he's thirsty."

I smile. "He always woke up in the middle of the night for one more feeding, and it stuck."

"Did you breastfeed him?"

I sigh, trying to give him pieces of the truth but instead I tell him the whole truth. "I tried, but Danny didn't like it because it meant I had to nurse him all the time and he thought my breasts would be ruined."

"That piece of shit told you that?" I nod. "What did you ever see in him, Alina? Is that why you have implants?" I flinch at his hard tone.

"Yeah, he made me get them."

"Made you?" He gets up, and I wince, knowing I said a little too much.

"He wasn't always like that. When I was pregnant, he wasn't so callous or controlling. He asked Joaquin if I could move with him so that I didn't have Maxim around the guys with the weed and different women."

"I get why Joaquin would agree but go back to the part where you said he made you."

My eyes slide up his naked chest with the swirls of beautiful ink to his handsome face.

"He threatened you, didn't he?"

"It's done. I got them, and I can't rip them off and the pain was too much to go back and reverse it, and besides, what I do for money, it isn't frowned upon."

"Come here." I walk up to him in my cotton pajamas and he tugs on my top. "Take it off."

I slide the cotton shorts down my legs and then lift my top over my head.

"I want you to sleep with me in my bed. Do you think you can do that for me?"

"Why?" I ask.

I know he said he can't give me more, but I want to know why now. Why this sudden change?

He presses a small kiss on my stomach. I don't hold his face. I don't run my fingers through his hair. Instead, I stay rooted to the spot. I know not to fall for it because like always, there is no future with him. That's been my plan all along—to leave when it's finally safe.

"Because you understand me, Alina. I'm sorry for bringing someone else while you and Maxim were here."

"You don't have to apologize; I just don't like Maxim listening and he had trouble falling asleep that night. You don't have to feel sorry for me."

"I don't feel sorry for you. I feel like I let you down somehow for leaving and not checking up on you. I don't want to argue or fight with you."

"Then don't."

"I want us to be friends."

"Then, we'll be friends."

I step back and walk around to the left side of the bed and slide in, giving him my back.

Little by little, I have to learn to let go. I have to learn to just be his friend and close my heart to him for good because it's been neglected and shitted on for the past six years.

Nineteen

ALEX

I stretch out to turn off the sound of the alarm going off from my cellphone. I look over, expecting to see Alina sleeping, only to find the bed empty. I look at the Tv monitor and only see the bed made. Alina always makes the bed when she and Maxim get up every morning. She cooks and cleans. I don't want her cleaning because I hire people to do that shit.

After washing up, I head to the kitchen and the smell of pancake batter hits me.

When I walk in, I see Maxim playing on his iPad and an Apple laptop's open on the other end. When I look over to the stove, my eyes take in the gorgeous woman in the shortest shorts on and one of my t-shirts that say Arizona Kings on it. I couldn't put Hillside Kings on the shirt so Arizona Kings was the safest to not attract too much attention.

I walk up behind her, placing my hands on her hips, and nuzzle my nose in her hair and say softly, "Good morning, *mi reina*."

She smiles. "Good morning."

"Hi, Smiley," Maxim greets me from the table.

I turn around and he is all smiles. "Hi, did you sleep well?"

"Did you?"

I turn my head looking at Alina and our eyes meet for a split second. "The best."

Having Alina next to me in bed was the best sleep I've had in a long time. It wasn't about sex and I didn't have to worry about kicking a chick out in the morning.

Which brings me to the next thing I need to talk to Alina about, but the laptop open on the dining table has me curious as to what she is looking at.

I turn it slightly and read the title of the open word document: Consumer Behavior in Marketing. Is she in school?

The front door opens, and in walks Hector, Julio, Carlito and five other members along with Leo and Katalia.

"Smiley! Donde estas cabron!" Hector calls out.

"Damn it smells like an IHOP in here," Carlito adds.

Leo and Katalia have grins plastered on their faces looking behind me.

"Shoot." I hear Alina. When I turn around, she is clenching her thighs and her back is to the counter. My eyes widen because I forgot what she was wearing and there is a bunch of single guys that just walked in.

I turn to Leo. "Get the guys out of here, carnal. Katalia can stay of course."

Leo chuckles. "Orale, cabron. Now I know why you haven't been stoppin' by the house to hang out."

Without another word, she bolts down the hallway.

"Are you two..." Katalia trails off.

I shake my head. "It's not what it looks like. We go way back. I've known Alina since I met Joaquin in high school with Khalani's brother, Ramon. Then Linda and I moved back here with Ramon and Khalani to branch out of L.A. Too many eyes over there and we need to protect the west of Hillside."

She nods. "So, if someone were to let's say ask her out on a date, you would be cool with it?"

I snort. "They would have to get through Joaquin first. She just got the shit knocked out of her recently, and in case you forgot, he's looking for her or more than likely waiting to do whatever sick shit he wants to do."

She looks at Maxim and he is engrossed playing a game on his tablet with his headphones on and then her eyes dart to me while I set the pan in the sink and turn on the water so it can cool off. "You're evading the question. I asked, would you mind?"

Of course I would mind. I would kill the fucker, but she deserves better than me. It would fuck with me, but we talked it out last night. We're friends.

"We're friends. As long as they treat her right, I'm okay with it."

Twenty

ALINA

I lean on the wall in the hallway, overhearing Katalia and Alex's conversation. I can't say I'm surprised to hear that he wouldn't care if I dated anyone. We're just two single people in a messed-up situation. I count to ten in my head and walk to the kitchen.

"Hey," I greet Katalia.

Katalia turns around and opens her bag to give me the brochure for the school her younger brother attends in West Hillside. Maxim begged me to see if he could go to the same school.

"Thanks. I'll look it over."

"I talked to Leo and he said they can accommodate him. The amounts are listed and the enrollment fees. We could help out if you want."

I smile, knowing she is just trying to help me out with Maxim. "That's okay. I'll figure it out."

"Figure what out?" Alex says after taking a bite out of the pancakes.

"Maxim and my brother hit it off, and Maxim is going to start school this year and I was giving her the brochure with the cost." Katalia turns to me. "I almost forgot. You would need to drive them because only the high school has transportation."

I bite my lip, knowing my car sucks right now. It's an hour's drive. Looking over at Maxim, my chest tightens because I don't think I can make this happen.

"Okay, I'll think about it. I appreciate all the information and for at least talking to the school."

"Don't thank me. I appreciate all the parenting books and tips you have been giving me," she says, rubbing her stomach self-consciously.

"How are you feeling?"

"Better. It was a rough go in the mornings, but I'm better. Luciana is going through it too."

"She's pregnant?" Alex asks.

"Yeah, I think I spoiled the surprise, but yeah, you know we have this pact that we wanted to have kids all at the same time so that we could all raise them together."

I tune out the whole pregnancy thing and sneak a peek at the cost of Maxim's school tuition. Thirty-one thousand without uniforms and supplies. The tuition alone is practically someone's salary. I have this semester to pay and next, and I'll done with my own tuition. I was planning to place him there for a year if I could get a good job after I graduate with my master's in marketing. I have ten thousand to pay before I can even think of paying two months ahead for Maxim.

I sit, resuming my paper.

"What's wrong?" Alex asks.

"Nothing, I have to finish this."

I do, but I don't want him to see that I'm trying to figure out my financial situation. It all circles back to the same thing. I can't afford to pay for Maxim to go to that school, and I can't let Katalia and Leo fit the bill. Maxim is my responsibility, not theirs.

"Why didn't you tell me you were in school?" Alex asks, leaning back in his chair.

"You never asked," I reply.

"What school?"

"UCLA online master's program."

"Damn, but I'm not surprised," Katalia says with a smile and slaps Alex playfully on the arm. "We Chicanas are smart too, ain't that right, *ese.*"

He nods.

Leo walks in and kisses Katalia on the head and turns to me. "Alina, Julio is asking if you're ready to take your car. Katalia and I will take Maxim so he can play at the house."

I shut my laptop, thankful for the interruption. "Oh, I almost forgot."

I give Maxim a kiss on the cheek, and he looks up. "Leo and Katalia are going to take you now, okay? Behave and don't give them any trouble."

"*Si, mama.* I'll be good. I promise." I press a kiss on his head and hand Katalia his bag with a change of clothes.

"Thank you, guys."

"Anytime," Leo says.

"Come over so you can hang out with us girls. We can go shopping."

"Yeah, sounds like fun."

I have no intention of doing any such thing. I don't belong in their world. I belong in the working class. The kind that lives on budgets and coupons. The struggling single mom's club. She has been so nice to me since coming here.

We come from similar backgrounds and share something in common—we both have been victims. It worked out for her though because of Leo and her Russian bratva leader, but me, I'm a Chicana that has no one except her little boy to raise.

Twenty-One

ALINA

I can hear the sound of machines going off in Julio's mechanic shop. It is located in the warehouse district in the east. I wasn't prepared to see all the classic cars being restored to their original beauty.

"This is amazing, Julio. Where did you learn?"

He smiles, opening the door and letting me through first. The office is a bit of a mess with piles of paperwork strewn all over the place. It smells like paper and rubber inside.

"My dad mostly. The rest with experience and time. The guys are going to have the starter installed and it should be ready in about thirty minutes."

He moves to get me a seat and swipes the chair with his bandana to get the dust off. The sun is already high in the sky casting a glow through the dusty windows.

"Thank you but you didn't have to go through all this trouble. I pull out my credit card and hand it to him. "Here, so you can charge me for the car."

He shakes his head. "No, I'm not going to charge you."

It's a credit card that is almost tapped out until my next payment but the parts must have cost him money.

"Charge me. At least for the parts."

He leans on the desk. "I'll only take payment based on a date."

He isn't giving up on the date thing.

"Are you serious?"

"Yeah. Dinner. Friday night."

"And you're so sure I'll say yes?" He looks away with a frown, and I feel bad because he is so nice to me. His head turns and his hands fidget with the bandana in his hands.

"I was hoping, eh?" He sighs. "Look, I'm not rich. I'm not a cartel king. I'm just a Chicano from El barrio that runs with the Kings and opened a shop to legitimize what he's made. I'm mechanic that fixes cars and wants to impress a woman that he thinks is amazing."

"You think I'm amazing?"

His expression goes soft. "You're the most beautiful woman I have ever seen. You're an excellent mother with a cool kid. I'm just asking for a chance to take you out."

Well, shit. I have never been asked out on a date before. I think about Alex and about last night. Joker, then the shower, and then this morning when he told Katalia that he didn't care if I moved on. Let go.

"Okay. I'll go."

"Y-you'll go. Are you saying yes?"

I grin and answer, "Yes."

He pushes off the desk with a smile. He starts firing off and he looks so cute. "What's your favorite restaurant or favorite food?" He slides his hand inside his front pocket. "I sound like a teenager going on his first date, don't I?"

"No, you sound perfect. I don't know any good restaurants and I like pizza, but if you really want this to go smoothly, I think you should ask my brother since you're a part of the Kings."

He slides his cellphone out and the screen lights up. "Right." He furrows his brows and asks me what I have been waiting for him to ask. "Are you and Smiley—"

"We're friends. That is all we are. You're not overstepping where he is concerned or anything like that. Smiley will always see me like his best friend's sister so that is why things may seem confusing. You know why I'm here and it has nothing to do with anything personal between Smiley and me." Not anymore. I point at the phone in his hand. He looks hesitant and I don't want to make him feel uncomfortable. "You don't have to go through all the trouble just to take me out. I've seen some really pretty girls that hang out with you guys, eh? I'm surprised you don't have a girlfriend somewhere. You seem like a nice guy and it looks like you're doing well for yourself. There aren't many *vatos* like you where I come from."

I'm giving him an out. He doesn't need the shit that I bring into his life. He should be having fun with a girl that doesn't have a kid to raise on her own or a psycho out to ruin her life because in his mind he thinks Smiley cares about me. If Danny only knew, Alex could care less.

"Thank you. That means a lot coming from you but I don't like any of the girls that hang around us." He comes closer and lifts my chin with his finger and says softly, "I'm not interested in them. I'm interested in you."

My cheeks flame. I have had guys try to kick it with me. Especially when they find out I dance at a strip club. It's like they automatically think I'm easy. But I've never had someone just say they're interested without trying to kiss me or make it obvious that the real reason is just for sex.

Of course, with Joker, nothing was a possibility so it really didn't matter. The only thing that matters is Maxim.

My eyes meet his honey colored ones. Julio has this cute vibe and the fact that he fixes classic cars just adds to his appeal. He's tall and lean. He doesn't have piercings like Alex and doesn't seem to be a player from what I've seen so far, but I need to let him know I'm not interested in a hookup if that is what he's after because he thinks I'm a lonely single mom.

"It's nice you think I'm amazing and that you're interested in me, Julio, but if you think you taking me out means that I'll sleep with you because I dance at a strip club or because I'm alone--"

He shakes his head, interrupting me. "You got it all wrong,

Alina. I don't want that. I-I mean if it comes to that, I'm okay with it. I'm a man, but even if it did, *Preciosa*, it wouldn't be a one-time thing. I'm interested in you and Maxim. I don't care who I ask or who I have to deal with as long as if it gets me you. I don't care that you dance or that you have a crazy psycho out to ruin your life. I'm willing to be whatever you want me to be, Alina." He takes my hand. "Think about it, okay? You don't have to say yes right now, but I will call Joaquin and do whatever I need to for him to be okay with it."

All I do is nod my chest feeling tight because no one has ever... wanted me and Maxim in their life like that.

Twenty-Two

ALEX

"How much was the tuition for Maxim?" I ask Leo. "I saw Alina look at the brochure like it was a snake hissing at her and she didn't even read what the school had to offer."

"Katalia tried to tell her we would pay it since there are no scholarships available. We could get him in of course, but for appearance reasons, we need to send them the money and she refused."

"I'll pay it, ese."

"It's only thirty-one thousand dollars."

"It will keep her from dancing to come up with it. I want to pay it. Also, ask Colton to find out how much her tuition is."

"Knight in shining armor. I like it, *cabron*. You know you can tell me and I won't say shit."

A chill runs down my spine at what he is implying. "What are you trying to ask, *puto*?"

He laughs. I'm in the passenger seat of his car, driving toward his house. Katalia left with Maxim and her bodyguards to their house. "I've known you for a long time, carnal. You cannot sit here and tell me you have not hit the culazo on that woman you have sleeping in the next room. No disrespect, *ese*, but Alina has a fat ass with the tits to go with it." He continues to laugh, and I want to smack him for busting my balls. He isn't stupid. None of the cartel kings are. "The poor vatos you deal with are trying so hard not to stare at her in the room; their eyes are about to stay stuck in their head from avoiding to look at her because they all know––you will murder them for so much as looking in her direction. I also heard what you did in the parking lot at the Satin Doll."

"I'm not saying shit. What we need to worry about is Joker and smoking that *puto* first."

The electronic black gate opens to his estate and he drives his SUV forward so I can wait for Alina to pick up Maxim.

He places the car in park in the driveway and turns to me one last time. "Joker is here in Arizona. You need to convince Alina to be careful, *ese*. We still don't know what he is planning. He is running with the dirtiest of the cartel in Mexico. Human trafficking and smuggling. I don't know about you, but Alina and Maxim aren't safe. People like that don't care about family and he obviously is willing to hurt her. He almost killed her."

Dread filters inside my chest at imagining her dead, and I'll never forgive myself if something happened to her. She doesn't deserve what life has dealt her. The only good thing in her life is the little boy that beams every time she walks in the room.

"Anything she needs for herself or Maxim comes out of my cut, you hear me? Don't tell her I paid for it. Tell Aiden to tell the board they gave him a scholarship or some shit to cover it up."

"You are definitely related to Mase. That is what he did for Luciana and her Porsche."

"Yeah, well. I'm not built for domestication."

"You are. You just have your head up your ass and won't accept what is right in front of you."

I snort. "I'll just put her life and her son's life in danger running the streets. I'm no good at being a husband or a father figure."

"Then don't run the street, *cabron*. You have enough money to build a house next to ours. You're a fucking multi-millionaire, Alex. Start acting like it. Let me ask you something and this is between you and me. Are you in love with Luciana?"

Do I love Luciana? Yes. Am I in love with Luciana? No. I knew the answer to that after I had sex with her the last time because I was willing to give her up. I realized she belonged with my cousin, Mase. There will always be a spark inside of her that belonged to him, and I made the right decision because I didn't feel like something was missing when she was with him.

"I'm going to tell you something I have never told anyone." He raises a brow because out of all the Kings, I keep my feelings bottled up. "When I'm in love with a woman, I don't share her with anyone because that woman is mine. And I'll kill anyone who touches her. I hope that answers your question."

"Damn, no sharing, huh?"

I roll my eyes and sigh. "No, fuckface. I don't want another cock inside my girl."

He knows what that means. There is no way I love Lucy if I shared her with Mase. It was me telling myself I was letting her go. It was me realizing I didn't love her like I thought I did.

Twenty-Three

ALINA

I pull in the driveway after leaving Julio's shop. He washed my car and let me know after he fixed the starter that he gave my car a full tune-up. He wanted to make sure the car wouldn't give me any trouble. Four of the other Kings followed me here and drove off when I turned on to the exclusive street on the west of Hillside making sure I made it safe.

I stop in front of Katalia and Leo's gorgeous mansion with tall green hedges that offer privacy. The house has those beautiful double doors with iron design built on frosted glass. Coming here is like stepping into another world where poverty doesn't exist. The cream-colored travertine marble is stunning with tiny veins of gray on the walkway. The door opens and there are two bodyguards that I recognize as little Niko's security detail from Katalia's agreement with the head of the bratva. She has to raise him, and the child is utterly the most beautiful child I have ever seen. He looks like Ken and Barbie's offspring.

"Hi, is Katalia home?"

They nod, probably only catching her name and don't understand a word I'm saying.

I walk in the open space with birch-colored flooring and white linen sofas to the open sliding doors that overlook the pool. The sound of Maxim giggling and the splash of water has my attention and my chest flutters.

Alex is playing with Maxim, squirting water guns. "You got me!" Alex calls out to Maxim.

He is wearing swim trunks and the drops of water run down his chest and is carrying a huge super soaker aiming it at Maxim. Maxim has two huge water balloons in his hands that look like bombs. Katalia's little brother and Leo hide behind a water feature that looks like a waterfall.

Movement catches my attention, and I smile when Katalia comes, carrying Niko. "They're having fun out there."

I nod but try to hide the fact that I was surprised Alex was here with Maxim and that I was ogling him while he played with my son, wishing for something that could never happen, like a glimpse of a dream you know could never come true.

"Niko looks like a magazine baby."

"He does. He is so good and feeding him a good meal allows me to sleep at night. Did you feel tired when you were pregnant with Maxim?"

"Yeah, all the time. You crave weird stuff like pickles and ketchup, but with me, it was pancakes. Maxim loves pancakes. It makes sense; he can't stop eating them."

"So does Smiley. I saw him scarfing down a stack of five." I laugh.

"Yeah, I should invest in a pancake house for both of them."

She holds Niko against her chest and nudges her head toward the pool.

"They've been going at it for three hours now. Did Julio fix the car?"

I caress Niko's soft hair with my fingers. "Yeah, he washed it and everything. He wouldn't let me pay either. He asked me out on a date as payment."

Katalia's eyes light up. "He did?"

I snicker. "Yeah."

"What did you say?"

I shrug my shoulders. "I didn't say anything. He said to think about it, but I'm not sure. I don't want my brother to go apeshit. Look at the mess I'm currently in."

Before she can say anything, our conversation is interrupted. The front door opens and the rest of their family walk in. Luciana, Mase, Khalani, and Aiden. The next generation of cartels working on the next one.

"Hey, you guys," Luciana beams as she comes up, closes her eyes, and inhales Niko's smell. "I can't wait."

Colton and Linda come next and they all greet each other.

"So, what's up?" Linda asks.

Katalia waits until the guys go out to the patio to shoot the shit with Leo and Alex. "Julio asked Alina out."

Linda glances at me. "Does Smiley know?"

Khalani gives me a smirk and says, "This is going to be so much fun."

"Did this *vato* ask Joaquin? You know your brother," Lucy adds.

I rub my arms nervously. " I told him about Joaquin and he said he was going to ask whoever he had to ask."

"Julio's hot. He got that LA cholo swag going on and it's cool that he fixes classic cars," Khalani says.

Linda looks over at Smiley still having a water fight while the other guys are getting soaked like little kids. "Go for it. You need some time too, Alina. Julio will treat you right. Maxim can stay here with Leo and Katalia after we go shopping."

"I know just the look too," Lucy says with excitement.

I bite my bottom lip. "I don't know."

"What's wrong?" Katalia asks.

I lift my hair off my neck like I'm hot but I'm just...nervous. "I know this sounds crazy, but I've never been out on a date like that."

They stop talking, and Khalani's eyes go soft. "But I thought Maxim's father–"

"Is an asshole. Joker turned out to be a sick bastard that only cares for himself and whatever agenda he is on." Linda says, "When did Julio want to take you out?"

"This Friday, but I haven't agreed to it yet."

Lucy's eyes widen. "Well, what are you waiting for? Call the *vato* so he can call your brother and get permission so Smiley doesn't go apeshit, but I think he will anyway."

I'm curious as to why she would think he would since they used to have something going on and he just told Katalia that he didn't. "I don't think Smiley would care if Joaquin were okay with it." They snort in tandem. "What?"

Lucy walks up to me. "What size? And your tits look amazing by the way."

My lip twitches. "They're fake."

"So are my mother's and it looks to me you had nice ones before. These are just...enhancements. Nice ones."

"I agree," Khalani says with a smile.

Katalia gives her a knowing look, and I clear my throat. "Thirty-four triple D."

"Nice. Okay, I'll get the dress. Linda will get the shoes. Katalia, hair and make-up, and Khalani will handle the thong."

Khalani leans close with a sultry smile. "And not just any thong. *The* thong."

"You guys are crazy."

"Nah, we are just plotting, but don't you worry, *carnalita*. This is all on us. He won't know what hit him."

"Julio?"

Lucy is typing on her phone. "Who?"

"Julio."

She waves her hand. "Oh, yeah. Him."

Why do I get the feeling there is something more at play here.

Katalia leaves with Niko, and after two minutes, comes back and throws a two-piece bikini at me. "Get dressed."

I hold the swim suit and raise a brow hoping it will fit.

Twenty-Four

ALEX

I noticed the second she walked in and saw me playing with Maxim. Every time she is close, I can feel her. She may not notice me, but I always notice her. When we were in high school, the guys would give me shit because my eyes were always glued to her ass. Alina was gifted a big ass and all that dancing has probably made it look like a nice peach.

She disappeared after the girls arrived, and my gaze keep going back to the house even though I'm trying to avoid getting hit.

I duck when I see a water balloon fly across my head. "*Higo de la Chiganda!* The fucker moved."

My head whips around at Mase. "Keep at it, *cabron*. I'm going to get you." I aim the gun and soak the fucker and wetting him some more watching his sunglasses fly off his head.

When he wipes his face, Maxim throws another one of his water balloons at his forehead. I laugh when I hear Maxim giggle. "Got 'em, Smiley. Did I do good?"

His little dimple pops out. The same one Alina has on her left cheek. The one I like to lick when I kiss her.

"Yeah, Maxim. You did good, *chavalo*."

"You're teaching him to have a good aim," Aiden says, while Mase is drying himself.

"He's good at everything. He's smart and funny," I praise. "I like him a lot and I don't even like kids, but if I had one—"

"Yeah, too bad his father is a dick. So why don't you hook up with his mom and keep him," Colton says when Marcus and Maxim are out of earshot.

"He isn't a pet, Colton," Aiden scolds. Then his bitch ass smiles when he glances at me. "He has a point. Are you sure you're not hitting that. Because we know you like her. Probably have fucked and you are hiding it from us. We aren't blind. You look at each other like you share this big secret."

"Why don't you take my sister and make me an uncle."

"Speaking of which, Lucy's pregnant."

"So is Linda."

"No shit. It works down there?" I tease Colton.

I fist-bump Colton, but when I glance at Aiden, he shakes his head. "Not yet, *puto*. I'm waiting for you."

I smile inwardly. I'm going to be an uncle to all my boys kids.

Leo walks in the pool, splashing water in his hair. "It's just you two fuckers. Let's kill that *hijo de la puta madre* Joker. Tell Joaquin you're raising his nephew, and that if he gets mad, you'll kill him and marry his sister anyway. Have babies. The end." He looks at Aiden. "Then get Khalani pregnant with twins. I'm still calling that one."

"Just because you have to marry your daughter to a Russian, don't get on me."

Mase laughs. "Hey, at least the little *vato* is good-looking."

"The kid has bodyguards since he was born."

"He's born to be a killer like all you fuckers," I say.

"*Este pinche cabron* acts like he's the nicer one of us. You blasted that fool in a parking lot because he talked shit to Alina. You didn't care who saw it," Colton says.

Lucy smiles when she comes out with Khalani in a swimsuit. I notice she has that glow women get when they're pregnant, and to her, it means more since she lost her first baby.

"How are you feeling? I heard the good news."

She smiles and it's the happiest I've ever seen her. "I'm going to have my second angel, Alex."

"I know, *Preciosa*. You're going to be an excellent mother."

She looks down at her stomach which looks a little bigger than before. She waves over to me. "Give me your hand."

I pinch my brows. "Why?"

"So the baby can meet its family."

"She made me do the same thing, *ese*," Colton says, filling up the other water gun.

"Fine." I hold out my hand, and she steps close in the shallow part of the pool and my hand is flat against the stomach. She talks to her baby that doesn't understand shit she is saying.

"You look awesome in the bikini, Alina," Katalia says. My gaze lands on the tips of her toes on the cool marble by the pool and my eyes trail up to her perfectly sculpted body and my throat goes dry. I tune out Lucy, and when my eyes reach Alina's, the look of sadness is like a knife to my heart.

Is she jealous? I'm sure they told her about me and Lucy, but there have been many women since then. It's not like I'm kissing her or screwing Lucy in the pool. But I don't miss that way she looks at my hand on Lucy's stomach or the way she places a fake smile and looks away toward Katalia, telling her thank you while she walks away with her phone.

My hand slides off Lucy's belly and the sound of a balloon smacking in my face snaps me out of it. It must be all in my mind because she is here and back in my life.

Twenty-Five

ALINA

I pull up the message app on my phone and text Julio.

Me: Do you still want to take me out?

Julio: I'll always want to take you out. Is that a yes?

I look up at Alex, and he is busy playing with the kids and the guys. Let go. I take a deep breath, smile, and let go.

Me: Yes. As long as it doesn't get you in trouble with the Kings.

Julio: I got the green light from your brother, but here, you're in control. I'll pick you up at seven on Friday. What's your favorite color?

Me: Red.

Julio: *Como las rosas.*

Me: Como el *corazon.* The heart and flowers usually come in the color red.

Julio: Red it is, then. I can't wait to see you, beautiful. Say hi to Maxim for me.

Me: I will.

I hear Katalia settling in the lounger next to me and turning her head. I look up from my phone and smile. "I got a date for Friday."

"You're nervous."

I'm unsure. I'm scared of everything but I have to be strong and be happy. I have to let go of my past and hope it doesn't catch up and finish destroying me.

I scrape my nail with my thumb, knowing I'm crossing a line. "Yeah, but I have to try and move on, right?"

"I did and it worked out. I know it will work out for you too. We are all here to help you. You know that, right? You're not alone."

"Thanks, Kat."

Twenty-Six

ALEX

"I need to talk to you."

Alina looks up from the computer. I wanted to talk to her about her work situation. She can't go to the club because Joker is in Arizona.

"About?"

Another one-word answer. It's been like this since earlier at the pool. Maxim is sleeping in the room. The little guy had a blast and fell asleep knocked out.

"Work."

"What about it? I have to go tonight. No exceptions."

"Alright. But you can't dance there."

"Why?"

"Because that *pinche desgraciado* is waiting to catch you alone, Alina."

She snorts. "I have bills to pay, Smiley."

"No, you have the Kings that have enough to wipe their asses with for ten generations."

"So what? It's their money, not mine. It makes me feel like I failed. Like I failed Maxim."

"Look, I get it, and I have a solution."

She leans back in her chair, causing her t-shirt to stretch over her huge breasts. "What kind of a solution?"

"If you want to dance, then you can dance, but privately for me in Leo's club. Private room. You can name your rate and I'll pay it."

She bursts out laughing. Her smile, and the way she tilts her head remind me of her son. "And what makes you think I'll take your offer?"

"It's better than dancing for strangers. It's safer and no one has to know. Except, for Leo. He will know because he owns the place. Katalia will probably be privy to it eventually but it's temporary until you graduate."

"A lap dance? Or a pole dance?"

I lean toward her and drag her chair toward me so that her legs are between mine. My eyes trail over her thighs and breasts. "Both, but only for me. I don't want to see you dance in a place like that. Ever."

"Just dancing."

"I'm not going to have sex with you for money, Alina. You're not a whore. You saw what I did to the last person who thought you were."

"I know." She cocks her head. "No sex."

"No sex, but I will touch you. I will watch you. Three times a week for an hour. You're mine. Unless something comes up."

Twenty-Seven

ALINA

When I try to move on and let go, Alex throws this on me. I know he is trying to help because I refuse to take anyone's money. Especially his.

"Why do you want to see me dance?"

"Because I want to see you dance," he volleys back.

I shake my head. "You're lying."

He smiles and says, "I want to know that I have you all to myself for a little while."

Nice try.

"Are you flirting with me?"

"Yeah. I am because I get to have something no one else has had."

"Oh yeah, and what is that?"

"A private dance from Dulce."

He says my stage name and it sounds so sexy on his lips.

My thoughts go to Julio and this Friday, but then I remember him saying he doesn't care that I dance. It is not like I'm cheating on anyone and I know Alex doesn't want anything serious. It is just foreplay for him.

I lean back and give him a hard stare. "I'll do it, but you have to tell me the truth of why you are offering to do it."

He frowns and leans back. "I told you why."

"No, you're telling me the version that makes it seem you're getting something out of it when we both know all you have to do is call one of the girls that show up to get laid. You don't need me to dance for you so you can have wild fantasies."

He sighs and leans his head back on the chair. "If I tell you the truth, you will agree to it no matter what I say next."

I knew it.

"Alright. If you tell me the truth, I'll do it."

He nods. "You know that Joker is in Arizona and the Kings think it is best that you lay low. Dancing in a room full of strangers is not possible when it's too risky and everyone knows you have turned them down for monetary help. So, I asked Leo for a room in his club. I get an hour to watch you instead of a bunch of strangers and your brother is cool with it because it is only one King instead of a bunch of us inside a club where anyone could come up and do something to hurt you. It's for your protection."

I swallow the thickness in my throat. Now it makes sense why Joaquin told Julio it was okay to ask me out, but I don't think Smiley knows that part.

"What are you guys doing on Friday?"

Alex scratches the back of his head and sighs, "We will all be at the meet up. Why?"

Julio and my brother didn't tell him. Good.

"No reason, just asking." I lean close to his ear. "Thank you for telling me the truth. I'll do it, but on one condition." He lifts his head to face me. "Don't touch me. No sex. We're friends, so let's not complicate things."

Twenty-Eight

ALINA

I drop Maxim off with Leo and Katalia since there is more protection, and besides, Maxim was ecstatic because her little brother is there and they're having a sleepover.

What I didn't count on was that Alex is taking me downtown in a black Mercedes sedan. The neon lights in the interior glow in blue, highlighting the dash like a gaming room.

"Whose car?" I ask.

"Mine."

"How many cars do you have?"

I've seen him in different classic cars, the G-wagon, and low-riders with colorful murals. I wonder where he keeps them all. I've only seen the G-Wagon and one of the classic cars at the house.

He grins. "I have more than most. Mainly, what I like."

"Oh, I was curious, that's all."

"Why?"

"Because you don't live like the other Kings from the west."

"I choose to live the way I do, Alina. I got used to it and I like helping the guys so why change things. My sister was my priority and she is happily married to Colton. I take care of the guys and their families. You know how it is, when you grow up with nothing."

"Are you happy?"

He stops at a red light and glances at me. "Yeah, I guess, but I'll be even more happy when I know you are safe."

I angle my head and look out the window. "Be careful, Smiley. Joker isn't a nice person."

"I'm not good either, Alina. Maybe to some but not to me. "I kill people for money, drugs, and guns. I think it's the other way around. Joker needs to worry about me and what I'm going to do."

We reach a tall building in the upscale part of downtown Arizona and drive down a dark alley where there is a gate. Once they see Alex's car approach, it opens and there are two men in suits waiting. One opens the door on my side and the other moves to open Alex's door.

"Bienvenido, *Patron*. The room is ready for you and your guest. If there is anything you need, let me know. Don Santos told us to remind you of the club rules for the lady and her exclusivity."

"I'll take care of it."

What does he mean rules for my exclusivity?

We walk down a dark hallway that has doors on each side. I stop when the man opens the door and waves with his hand and says, "Let us know when you're finished, Patron."

I take in the room. The stripper pole in the center with a shiny black platform as a stage. Red carpet, lights lining the baseboards, and a black velvet loveseat and a chair.

Alex hands me a tablet with a music app and controls for the lighting system. "It's your set and your show. I'm just a spectator. The door to the back has an outfit for you to wear."

"Does it matter what I wear?"

"If I have to stare at you for the next hour, yes. I want you to wear what is in the room." He walks over and retrieves a black velvet box. "This is a sex club and there are rules. Mafia men and women are exclusive members here so if they see a woman without a collar, it means she doesn't have a Dom."

I smile sarcastically. "I don't have one."'

"While you're in here with me, you do."

I look around. "Where is he?"

He opens the black velvet box and there is a choker with paved diamonds four inches thick with red stones that reads CORTEZ. "Very funny."

"Turn around, Alina." I lift my hair and turn around, and while he wraps the choker on my neck, he says, "Don't take this off until you leave here, and when you arrive, make sure it is on. Do you understand, Alina? This not a game. There are very dangerous people that visit this place."

"I understand."

I don't need anymore trouble. I have enough going on right now. I guess that is what the man in the suit when we arrived meant by exclusivity.

I hold the tablet in my hand and scroll through the music selecting something that would fit the mood.

I walk out after changing into lingerie from Agent Provocateur. My eyes almost bugged out of my skull when I saw the price tag. Four hundred dollars for just the thong.

I glance to see his reaction when I grip my legs on the pole holding my body and flare out my arms.

His eyes watch every movement and every twirl like we're dancing together.

Tears sting the back of my eyes, and my heart opens, releasing my feelings for him. Letting him watch me shed his love like a snake releasing the skin of the past as he listens to the playlist of every song Romeo has written of lost love. A purging of our existence, making room for the one that deserves it. Letting go.

No more forbidden touches, no stolen moments, or kisses. No more fantasies of a man that lives his life happy without me while I live a life of suffering. Yearning for a love that doesn't exist.

My heels hit the platform and my back his to him. I blink back the moisture in my eyes so I can face him to give him a lap dance.

When I finally face him, he is still seated in the middle of the velvet couch. His shirt is off and his flat stomach ripples with muscle under the ink. I straddle his lap and grind my hips.

His breath hitches, I can feel hard he is, but his hands are spread on the back of the couch. His eyes follow my movements and when he finally reaches my eyes, he says softly, "You're beautiful."

But I don't answer. I let the compliment roll off my skin because there were many times I wished he said it, but never did I ever wish it was because he was forced to be around me. It's not real. This isn't real.

He's hard because he is a man and there is a half-naked stripper in his lap.

My long hair hides my face and it's like I'm looking at him through a screen.

"Alina?"

"Yeah."

"Has a man ever told you that he loves you?"

When the songs ends, I look at him. "Maybe someday," I say softly, pushing away and heading back to the changing room.

Twenty-Nine

ALEX

T drop Maxim off with Leo and Katalia since there is more protection, and besides, Maxim was ecstatic because her little brother Marcus is there and they're having a sleepover.

What I didn't count on was that Alex is taking me downtown in a black Mercedes sedan. The neon lights in the interior glow in blue, highlighting the dash like a gaming room.

"Whose car?" I ask.

"Mine."

"How many cars do you have?"

I've seen him in different classic cars, the G-wagon, and low-riders with colorful murals. I wonder where he keeps them all. I've only seen the G-Wagon and one of the classic cars at the house.

He grins. "I have more than most. Mainly, what I like."

"Oh, I was curious, that's all."

"Why?"

"Because you don't live like the other Kings from the west."

"I choose to live the way I do, Alina. I got used to it and I like helping the guys so why change things. My sister was my priority and she is happily married to Colton. I take care of the guys and their families. You know how it is, when you grow up with nothing."

"Are you happy?"

He stops at a red light and glances at me. "Yeah, I guess, but I'll be even more happy when I know you are safe."

I angle my head and look out the window. "Be careful, Smiley. Joker isn't a nice person."

"I'm not good either, Alina. Maybe to some but not to me. "I kill people for money, drugs, and guns. I think it's the other way around. Joker needs to worry about me and what I'm going to do."

We reach a tall building in the upscale part of downtown Arizona and drive down a dark alley where there is a gate. Once they see Alex's car approach, it opens and there are two men in suits waiting. One opens the door on my side and the other moves to open Alex's door.

"*Bienvenido, Patron*. The room is ready for you and your guest. If there is anything you need, let me know. Don Santos told us to remind you of the club rules for the lady and her exclusivity."

"I'll take care of it."

What does he mean rules for my exclusivity?

We walk down a dark hallway that has doors on each side. I stop when the man opens the door and waves with his hand and says, "Let us know when you're finished, Patron."

I take in the room. The stripper pole in the center with a shiny black platform as a stage. Red carpet, lights lining the baseboards, and a black velvet loveseat and a chair.

Alex hands me a tablet with a music app and controls for the lighting system. "It's your set and your show. I'm just a spectator. The door to the back has an outfit for you to wear."

"Does it matter what I wear?"

"If I have to stare at you for the next hour, yes. I want you to wear what is in the room." He walks over and retrieves a black velvet box. "This is a sex club and there are rules. Mafia men and women are exclusive members here so if they see a woman without a collar, it means she doesn't have a Dom."

I smile sarcastically. "I don't have one."'

"While you're in here with me, you do."

I look around. "Where is he?"

He opens the black velvet box and there is a choker with paved diamonds four inches thick with red stones that reads CORTEZ. "Very funny."

"Turn around, Alina." I lift my hair and turn around, and while he wraps the choker on my neck, he says, "Don't take this off until you leave here, and when you arrive, make sure it is on. Do you understand, Alina? This not a game. There are very dangerous people that visit this place."

"I understand."

I don't need anymore trouble. I have enough going on right now. I guess that is what the man in the suit when we arrived meant by exclusivity.

I hold the tablet in my hand and scroll through the music selecting something that would fit the mood.

I walk out after changing into lingerie from Agent Provocateur. My eyes almost bugged out of my skull when I saw the price tag. Four hundred dollars for just the thong.

I glance to see his reaction when I grip my legs on the pole holding my body and flare out my arms.

His eyes watch every movement and every twirl like we're dancing together.

Tears sting the back of my eyes, and my heart opens, releasing my feelings for him. Letting him watch me shed his love like a snake releasing the skin of the past as he listens to the playlist of every song Romeo has written of lost love. A purging of our existence, making room for the one that deserves it. Letting go.

No more forbidden touches, no stolen moments, or kisses. No more fantasies of a man that lives his life happy without me while I live a life of suffering. Yearning for a love that doesn't exist.

My heels hit the platform and my back his to him. I blink back the moisture in my eyes so I can face him to give him a lap dance.

When I finally face him, he is still seated in the middle of the velvet couch. His shirt is off and his flat stomach ripples with muscle under the ink. I straddle his lap and grind my hips.

His breath hitches, I can feel hard he is, but his hands are spread on the back of the couch. His eyes follow my movements and when he finally reaches my eyes, he says softly, "You're beautiful."

But I don't answer. I let the compliment roll off my skin because there were many times I wished he said it, but never did I ever wish it was because he was forced to be around me. It's not real. This isn't real.

He's hard because he is a man and there is a half-naked stripper in his lap.

My long hair hides my face and it's like I'm looking at him through a screen.

"Alina?"

"Yeah."

"Has a man ever told you that he loves you?"

When the songs ends, I look at him. "Maybe someday," I say softly, pushing away and heading back to the changing room.

..·║♛║·..

We're on the way to the meet up, but Carlito wants to stop to pick up some food on the way there. I keep looking at my phone, and I'm tempted to text Alina, but that would be a dick move. She's on a date with a guy who will treat her better than me. I think of her and Maxim leaving the house, and I can't imagine the house without them in it.

"You're in love with her, aren't you, *cabron*?" Hector asks.

I look over at Hector from the passenger seat and silently nod.

"Does she know?"

"It doesn't matter. I don't deserve her."

I think of all the years of not contacting her. The way I ignored her. I fucked another girl while she listened in the other room. I'm the biggest piece of shit next to the other asshole that beat her. I never took her out on a date, gave her flowers, or told her how amazing she is or how much I love when she smiles.

Hector pulls the Impala into the parking lot, and I frown. There are two unmarked SUVs.

"Go! It's the cartel and it's not the kind that runs with us." Hector tries to back out, but the guys in the car behind us are blocked by two more SUVs. "Fuck!" I yell banging my hand on the dash.

I pull out both my pistols, but a tap on my window grabs my attention.

The man waves at me with his gun to get out of the car. I close my eyes briefly but I was able to send a text to Mase.

I open the door and slide out. There are twelve men to our six and when I look over there are ten more with guns aimed at the other Kings.

"Nice night, isn't it?" I look over and Joker is standing with a hoodie over his head. I can see that he covered the Hillside King's tattoo with an image of a joker.

"*Estas loco. Te van a matar, pendejo,*" I say. "They're going to kill you when they come."

He laughs, and I swear I want to take my time when I finally get him. I'm going to kill him slowly, drawing out the pain so he can break over and over.

Joker rolls his shoulders and smiles. "I'm not here to kill you. Not yet anyway. I came here to talk."

"If this is about Alina--" He laughs, cutting me off.

I lean on the hood of the car, facing him with my pistol in my hand. He knows I won't open fire because that will leave the rest of my guys at risk to die.

"On your knees," he says to the rest.

"They comply when I nod."

"What the fuck do you want?"

"I want to watch you suffer before I kill you. This has always been about you. *Eres un estupido embecil.* I want your boys to know what a piece of shit you really are and how stupid you look when I break you, *pendejo.*"

My nostrils flare in anger, but I'm curious. "How do you plan on breaking me?"

"I promise this will break you the same way I've been breaking your girl all these years."

At the mention of Alina, I cock both my pistols and aim it at him, shaking in a blinding rage.

He chuckles. "You were always a loose fuse when it came to that woman, but I have secrets to share now that we have an audience. Show and tell."

"Fuck you, *puto*." I spit.

"Put the gun down or I'll have someone shoot your girl right now in the head. She's out on a little date, isn't she? Blood-red dress. You wouldn't want to bury her like your mother, would you? Her son without a mother just like you."

Something isn't right. He keeps calling her my girl.

The blood is pumping in my veins. I look over at the guys and they are watching.

"What do you want?"

He lifts his gun and looks at like he's admiring the metal. "To hurt you where you'll hurt most. What you are afraid to have. Afraid to acknowledge because you're pathetic and weak. A blind *pendejo* that doesn't care about his family. Especially, the girl whose cherry you popped at seventeen." All the guys snap their attention at me with their eyebrows raised. "But I fucked her until she cried because her baby daddy was too busy fucking every *hyna* from L.A. to Arizona."

"Motherfucker!" I scream. My vision blurs. "You're lying!"

"She cried so good, Smiley. She took it like a champ. Every thrust and every hit...all for you." *No. It can't be.* Tears slide down my cheeks at his admission. He continues, "I have never seen a woman love a man that much. She made sure she kept all your dirty little secrets while you slept good at night. You should be thanking me for the nice tits I made her get, but I made sure she posed nude while I took the pictures for everyone in the cartel to jerk off too." I think I'm about to throw up. "They made you a King, while I made her my whore."

Bile rises up my throat, and I close my eyes to clear my vision.

He gets closer, and I want to gut him the way he is gutting me with his words.

I'm so sorry, baby.

Joker taps my shoulder. "Relax, but the best part is the fact that you never raised your son. You were never there to watch him take his first step. Hear his first word. All while you are playing the leader like you wanted while your family suffered and your girl twirled on a pole for a buck. I wanted to make sure I took it all from you. You thought you were better than me. Better than everyone else because you were the pretty boy. The Don." He sucks his teeth. "I waited this long so that I could make sure she would hate you. She knew not to ask anything from you because she knew what would happen if she opened her mouth. And let me tell you, she has a nice mouth. Her cunt...is even better. And her tears...taste like heaven."

I try to lunge at him, but the man has the gun digging in my temple. Joker claps his hands together like he is giving a round of applause. "What do you say, Kings? Your leader is a great father that never took care of his family."

"Kill me, but leave Alina and my son alone."

"Your son?" He laughs, tapping the gun on his head. "If I was your son, I would be ashamed to have a father like you. Come to think of it, I think looking at his mother's face should be enough for your son to not ever consider you more than a low life that left them. Now that I have given you something to look forward to, like knowing the mother of your child shows her tits and pussy to strangers to feed your son, I'll leave you to it until I come back and finish your miserable life or meet your baby momma for a quickie like the last time she escaped you."

My eyes flick to his, and my lip curls. *Motherfucker!*

"Oh, she didn't tell you about my little visit? She's such a loyal whore. Because we both know she hasn't let you stick your infested cock in her."

That's why she was crying that night.

"Fuck you, *puto*." I get hit with the back of the gun across my head. The pain radiating through my skull has me gritting my teeth.

I get thrown to the ground and kicked in the stomach, knocking the wind out of me, causing me to struggle trying to take my next breath. Then they drive off. The roar of a car's engine from a distance comes flying through the parking lot. My vision blurs and I try to blink so I can focus.

I hear footsteps.

"Get Alina," I croak, and everything goes dark.

Thirty

ALEX

The night is perfect except the look on Alex's face when he saw Julio pick me up tonight. He looked defeated, and I honestly don't understand why. I thought it was because he felt Julio went behind his back, but when he asked me why, it was obvious it wasn't that.

"I think Smiley is in love with you," Julio says.

I scoff. "I told you we're just friends. Smiley doesn't love me like that. He's always seen me as a friend because of my brother."

I look at the gourmet pizza in the nice Italian restaurant Julio has taken me to.

"Alina?"

"Yeah."

"It's okay if you are. I'm not going to sit here and say I would be happy about it with the way you look at him when you think no one is looking but I want to tell you that he looks at you the same way."

I look through the glass windows behind him and I see two black SUVs pull up. I swallow and look at Julio when men with cowboy hats, jeans, and belt buckles jump out at the same time.

He must see the expression on my face because he asks, "Alina what's wrong?"

"Whatever happens next, don't fight it. Let them take me," I say quietly.

He looks over when the hostess tries to stop the men from barging in the restaurant. He yells, "Alina, run."

"They will kill you. Let them take me."

He gets up, causing the cups to fall on the table. I know I'm fucked. These men work for the Mexican cartel. Maxim is safe with Katalia and that is all that matters.

Two men walk behind me and two stand behind Julio. "*Que quieres*?" Julio asks. What do you want?

The man with the mustache walks forward, rubbing his jaw. "We're here for the *senorita*. She belongs to the cartel. You're a very smart woman. Brave even. Anyone would be cowering in fear, but you sit here, knowing you're outnumbered. Don't fight me and I won't have a restrain you."

"Where are you taking me?"

"Someone very important needs to speak to you. I don't like to keep him waiting."

"Don't hurt him, and I'll go willingly."

He nods. "Very well." He leans close and says to Julio, "Don't try anything. The man I work for doesn't like interruptions of any kind."

Julio clenches his jaw. His hands are fisted on the table, and I look at him pleadingly to cooperate.

⋯♔⋯

I'm sitting in the back of the SUV and the driver is driving south toward the border. "Where are you taking me?"

"Mexico."

"Who's your boss?"

He smiles, and I notice one of his front teeth have a gold cap. I squeeze my legs together and dread snakes up my spine when I notice he's looking at me. He turns, and I jolt when he reaches behind him and hands me a blanket.

"Thank you."

"I work for the Cortez Cartel."

After driving for three hours, we cross the border into Mexico. The car drives through mountain terrain, causing the car to sway and dust to cloud the windshield.

When we reach a huge hacienda, I know we have arrived. He said Cortez and that means it's Alex's father.

I'm escorted inside and an older woman greets me with a cold glass of water. "Alina, mucho gusto," she says with a smile. "*Me llamo, Juanita.*"

I give her a wry smile in return, taking the glass and seeing that it is clear and it doesn't look like it's laced with anything. I take a sip because my throat is dry and I'm shaking.

The man that brought me here walks up. "Right this way," he says in broken English.

I follow him until we reach a study with Mexican tiles that continue inside the room from the front. The walls are a pale white with brown wood shelves and a huge map of Mexico framed on the wall behind a man with hard black eyes seated behind a huge wood desk. "Have a seat, Miss Flores."

I'm not surprised he knows my name. Growing up on the streets of L.A., everyone that lives on a street full of Mexican gangs has heard of the cartel.

"How can I help you?"

He smiles, and I notice he has a mustache that is graying on the ends from age and has Alex's same color of eyes, dark with a hint of brown in the center.

He leans back in his leather chair and studies me. His eyes roam over every inch of my body, and I'm not sure whether to cringe or scream. "My son has excellent taste in women. Something he inherited from this side of the family, and it has come to my attention that you have a child that so happens to be my grandson. My blood."

Shit. He knows.

This is one of the reasons I remained silent about Maxim. He will be cast into a world of death, drugs, and money. He's innocent and full of life. The last thing I want is for him to follow in this man's footsteps.

"You don't know that for sure."

He chuckles. "I know for sure or you wouldn't be here. The same way I know Alex Cortez is my son. My blood. I'm going to be frank, Miss Flores. You either become my son's wife or his whore."

My lip curls in disgust. "Your son doesn't want a wife and has plenty of whores."

"I don't think you understand. You don't have a choice. If my son doesn't want a wife"—he tilts his head from side to side—"it's not a requirement from me. Cortez men always use protection. We don't slip unless it's someone we love. The same way I loved his mother." He places his hands on the edge of the desk and leans forward. "The rest don't mean anything. So, which is it?"

"I think you need to discuss your plans with your son and his whores and leave me and my son out of it. I'm not interested in being anything."

"Is that why I found you with another man at a restaurant?"

Now I'm pissed off. "Who I fuck and who I'm with is none of your concern, and Alex's even less."

He shakes his head and waves his hand. "I know about that *pinche hijo del la chingada* Joker. A sicario. He made you pay crimes for which he no right to make you pay. He visited my son today." I lower my head with a frown, hoping Alex is okay. "He told him everything he did to you and pistol-whipped my son for fun, laughing at him for manipulating the situation using another cartel as leverage to degrade you. I let him get away with it because I think it's my son's duty to clean up his mess. And to be honest, it is a good way to unleash the monster I know he really is inside. The monster he keeps locked up but all it takes is the right push. You are the reason, *Princessa*."

He looks at his watch, and I let the fact that Alex knows about my big secret and Maxim sink in. He will probably hate me for keeping Maxim from him but I did it to protect both of them. He may not want me but I did all of it...for them.

One of his men walks up behind me and announces, "He's ready."

Alex's father stands. "Alex is here and he's a little banged up. I think you should tend to him."

Dread settles in my veins. My heart pounds as I follow him out into the hallway. He leads me to a staircase, leading up to a room with double doors. "He's conscious. He has a head wound and what looks like a broken rib, but he'll live. It just shows how important my grandson is if something were to happen to my son. Think about that, Miss Flores, because if you don't agree, I'm afraid you will have to leave without your son because he is cartel by blood. I advise you to choose wisely. There is no room for regrets later."

Bastard.

When I think I'm made the sacrifices to save Maxim, it's like a cruel joke and I'm the star in it.

When I enter the room, there is a large Alaskan king-sized bed with Alex in it. There is a man taking his vital signs and a nurse cleaning up his head wound with gauze.

I step closer, my heels the only sound in the room. The doctor looks up when he sees me approach the edge of the mattress and removes the stethoscope. My eyes travel to the wound on his head and fear claws at my insides.

"He has a large gash that has been stitched up and a broken rib. He needs to rest for a about six weeks and he should heal. I've given him pain meds. He was unconscious for a bit but I think it was more from the adrenaline. He was upset and kept asking for you. I'm assuming you are Alina?" I nod. "He kept saying your name and I think something along the lines of him wanting to make sure you're safe. I think you should stay with him so he can rest."

"Okay, thank you." I look at the nurse. *"Gracias."*

"Si, Mrs. Cortez."

I don't correct her. In their eyes, I belong to Alex as his wife.

Thirty-One

ALEX

I wince at the sharp pain on the right side of my head.

"Shh, I'm here." I hear the sound of Alina's soft voice, and I hope I'm not dreaming. "I'm here, Alex."

My eyes focus on the ceiling with the Mexican mural, and I know I'm in Mexico. I can smell the difference in the room I'm in. The air is different. Foreign. The only thing familiar is the sound of her voice.

"Alina," I croak.

The bed dips beside me, but I can't turn my head. It feels like someone busted it open with an ax. Her face pops up in front of me.

Her dark hair falls over my bare chest. "You're safe."

She nods. "I am, but you're hurt and you need to rest."

"Don't leave me. Please?"

"I'll stay until you get better."

I close my eyes. Everything feels heavy and I drift off to sleep.

When I open them again, it feels like I closed them for just a second but I know better. I must have been asleep for hours. I look down and smile when I see Alina's head lying on my chest. I press a soft kiss on her forehead.

"She's beautiful." My father's voice comes from my right.

I turn my head to the right and I find him standing at the double doors that lead to my room.

" She is but I've also failed her. I've failed our son. It is something I can't take back."

"Then do something about it."

"How?" My eyes snap to him. "How do I erase the time she has had to spread her legs because of me and the abuse. How do I get back the time that has been taken away, Papa. How do I show her how incredibly sorry I am. I've hurt her in so many ways. I can't look at her, knowing what I've done."

"You wouldn't have done it had you known."

"Yeah, because I was too busy getting my dick sucked while an innocent woman and her son were struggling, and the mother of my son, abused and degraded like a whore."

I think about all the things she has learned about me. Lucy and all the wealth I've acquired. She watched me live my life while she was trapped in a nightmare because of me. Because I was a coward and didn't want to face my best friend out of loyalty. In the end, she and Maxim paid the price.

"Then fix it. You don't want to marry, then fine, but she stays. She will always be the mother to your son, Alex. Make sure she is the only one that is. Fuck whoever you want but she will be the mother to your children."

I clench my teeth, not wanting to wake her up or raise my voice. "That is not your decision to make."

"I'm afraid it is. The little boy has your blood in his veins and the last thing I think you want is for him to grow up without his mother. Things like that creates monsters that can't be controlled. Alina Flores is tied to the cartel whether you like it or not. There is no escaping that, *hijo*. Nothing matters except staying alive because that *payaso* out there wants you dead and is playing with your head to break you. I could send him to be killed but I think you want vengeance for yourself."

"Send me back home to my apartment in Downtown Arizona. Maxim starts school and he is not used to being without Alina for more than a day. I'll let you know what I decide, but Alina and Maxim come first."

"It's about time you take your rightful place."

<h1>Thirty-Two</h1>

ALINA

The next morning, I'm awaken by one of the staff at Alex's father's house. They escorted Alex with two men helping inside a private plane after giving him a dose of painkillers.

"Where are we going?"

"My house."

"I need to pick up Maxim."

"Don't worry. I already called Leo and I know Katalia told you he was having fun at the zoo. School starts soon?"

"Yes, I have to drop off the paperwork at the public school."

His head lifts and his eyes are unreadable when he says, "Maxim is not going to a public school, Alina. I paid for him to attend the private school with Katalia's brother like he wanted. Whatever you or Maxim need will be provided. I have lost valuable time with my son and I would like to get to know him better than I already have. It is all I ask, Alina."

"Of course. I'm sorry. I didn't—"

He interrupts me by holding his hand up. "Shh, save it. I don't want your apology. I want your obedience when it comes to him and what I ask of you. You're mine, Alina, and there is nothing you can do to change that."

He must be high on his meds. I'm not his just because now he knows that I've had this secret love child I have kept hidden all these years.

Glancing in his direction causes fear to snake up my spine because he won't look at me the same. He's distant and I think Joker succeeded in breaking Alex because the man in front of me is not the same one I left on Friday. This man is a narco. A ruthless leader that is hard and cold, caring only for one thing, to cause death and destroy whoever is in his way, and I hope that doesn't include me.

When the plane lands, we are escorted in black sedan to a tall building in the downtown.

The doors open and there are two bodyguards waiting at the entrance of the building that looks like luxury apartments housing one on each floor.

"You live here?"

"You know where I live, Alina. If you're asking I own an apartment in this building, the answer is yes. I also own part of the building."

"I can leave, Smiley."

He bows his head and laughs trying not to wince from the discomfort. "I'm not Smiley to you, Alina. When you address me, you call me by my name, and no, you're not leaving. You'll stay because my son stays with me and that is non-negotiable. *Entiendes*?"

I nod because what fucking choice do I have. I'm fucked. Letting him go or not doesn't change the fact that I'm tied to him and his family now. There are no more secrets and no more hiding who I was to Alex or who Maxim's father is.

"What are you going to tell Joaquin?"

He presses the elevator and the sound of it opening is all that I hear as I wait for him to answer my question.

He grimaces when he walks into the elevator slowly.

"The truth. That I slept with his sister and got her pregnant and she had my son. He has two choices, to get over it or not. It doesn't matter. There is nothing he can do about it."

I wince because the way he says it is like a circumstance he regrets being part of.

"I'm sorry you feel that way."

The elevator doors ping open. "I have nothing to feel sorry for, Alina. Maxim is perfect. Now I have to do the right thing and be there."

He walks ahead of me, careful not to make sudden movements. The gauze that is taped to the wound of his head needs to be changed, and I need a hot shower before Maxim arrives. We have to explain what happened to the man that he thinks is his uncle's friend.

Then, I remember that I don't have any clothes and I'm still wearing the silk dress from my date with Julio. He has been calling me non-stop, but I haven't answered. How could I explain what happened when I can't even explain to the man who deserved to know all these years that he had a son. Alex must be angry and disgusted with me and I can't blame him. He lost time and precious moments with Maxim that he can't get back.

"I need to get back to the house to pick up some clothes. I would like to take a shower and I need to change your dressing."

There is a bag he places on the countertop by the kitchen, and I know it has the items I would need to clean the wound.

He turns and says, "Take off your dress, Alina."

"W-what?" I ask, confused.

"I'm not going to ask twice. Take it off and go to the bedroom," he says in a hard tone.

I walk toward the bedroom but fully clothed. When I reach the massive bedroom the size of the living room, I notice the huge bed with white sheets.

He enters and undoes the zipper of his jacket and slides it off in a heap on the floor. I move to pick it up, but his voice echoes in the large room.

"Leave it."

"Why?"

"Because I hire people to do that shit for me. I have better things for you to do."

"Like what, dance?" I challenge.

He smirks. "Oh, you will dance for me. You will do everything I ask from now on.

"Or what?"

"I'll make you do it anyway."

I snort. "Good luck with that. You're in no condition to demand shit, *cabron*."

He grins. "Then you don't know me, *muneca*." He swallows. "Come and clean me up."

I walk to the bathroom and hold the door open. I prepare the shower, but I pause when I see toiletries unopened on the counter.

I look over when he walks in.

"I took the liberty to bringing all of your stuff over here."

I pick up a face cream that I've seen on a magazine when I go to my doctor's appointments for my birth control refills. "This stuff is expensive."

"And?"

"And I don't need it because my face has been fine without it."

He rolls his eyes. "Thank you would have been nice."

I sigh. "Thank you, but you don't have to."

"Get used to it, Alina. Bitch at me later. But right now, I really want a shower. Can you take off the dress and get in with me. I can't wash my dick."

I almost choke on my spit. He wants me to bathe him. This should be fun.

I take a handful of body wash and lather his skin, careful to be gentle where his ribs are broken. He keeps his head from getting wet, but I have no choice but to remove the bandage. It is getting soaked form the water.

When I get to his cock, it grows hard in my hand, and I look up to see his eyes watching my hands as I stroke the length of it from the base to tip.

"Get on your knees," he demands.

"Alex—"

"Get on your knees, Alina." I get on my knees and look up at his handsome face. "Give me your mouth."

His tongue peeks out, and I glance at his thick veiny cock with the piercing on the tip, wondering how the middle would feel gliding across my tongue.

After I wash him. I wrap my hand around his hard shaft and slide my tongue across his length until I suck the head inside my mouth.

He closes his eyes. "Fuck, Alina."

I take him in my mouth and slide his cock until he reaches the back of my throat.

Tears slide down my cheeks.

I suck like it is the most delicious thing I've tasted.

"I'm going to come, Alina. Do you know why I call you by your name instead of *Preciosa* or *muneca* all the time, huh?" My eyes flick to his, and his nostrils flare when I don't stop. I taste the saltiness of him on my tongue, and I moan. He's close. I can feel it.

He bites his bottom lip, and the skin pinches between his brows as he slides his fingers in the wet strands of my hair. I shake my head, because honestly, I don't.

"It's because I love the way it rolls of my tongue, the same way it felt when I came inside you and you gifted me our son," He rasps, while hot strings of come slide down my throat, and I drink him in. "Fucking perfect. Look at me." Her eyes lift. "The only tears you will cry from now on is when my cock is down your throat."

Tears flow freely down my chin because the pain of his rejection still lives inside my heart mixed with the love I have held on to for so long, trying to shed it out of me. I'm on my knees because I'm still weak for him. He may say things when he's high on lust, but the truth will always remain the same—Alex never loved me.

Thirty-Three

ALEX

After our shower, she applies the ointment to help with the healing on my stitches and we fall asleep on the bed to get some rest before Leo and Katalia arrive with Maxim. I don't know what to do or say but I see the look in her eyes and I know she was ready to let me go. She wants to move on from me but I'm the one pulling the strings and keeping her here. She would have left if I didn't practically force her to stay using Maxim as the reason.

I'm scared to lose her for good.

If I let Alina walk out of the door with my son, all I would get are visitation rights, while some *vato* like Julio gets the best part of her.

She stirs on my chest, the soft comforter slipping down her back and giving me a glimpse of the curve of her waist.

The front door beeps, and I know it's Leo because he's the only one that would show up right now expecting him to bring Maxim. Only the Kings have access to my penthouse in the city.

When he reaches the threshold, he raises he eyebrows. "Damn, *ese*. All banged up and you still manage to get some," he says with a big smile, placing his sunglasses on his head. "We all knew you two had something going on."

I grin. "Where's Maxim?"

"He's coming. Katalia took him shopping and got him stuff for his new room."

I never thought I would use the second room in this apartment. I sold the last one after Linda married Colton because it was intended for her in case something happened but then the Kings invested in this building offering each of us a penthouse, I jumped on the opportunity.

I caress Alina's back, careful not to let the blanket slip because we are both naked.

"I need to thank her. She's great with him and her brother."

"Yeah, she and the girls are going crazy buying baby shit and now that we all know Maxim is your son, they are going nuts, *cabron*. You have to help stop the madness. Mase is losing it with the shopping. Lucy is on a spending spree."

I chuckle.

"Who pays eighteen thousand dollars on a crib. Who?"

"A cartel queen named Lucy."

"Now tell me, how are you feeling?"

"Like I got the shit kicked out of me. I'm trying to figure out how to get better faster so I can go find that asshole."

"I think you should take the time to work on other stuff first before going apeshit on that asshole."

"Yeah, I know."

I need to make up for lost time.

Thirty-Four

ALINA

I hit submit on my last assignment for the semester. One more semester to go. I log in and check the payment schedule. I repeatedly refresh the page when it keeps saying I have a zero balance. I look into the school account ledger for a history of payments and I see there were two payments made last week, covering all of my tuition until I graduate.

I get up and walk into the master bedroom. Maxim was so tired; he was practically asleep when he arrived with Katalia that I put him down in the second bedroom. Overnight, the kid now has multiple bedrooms when I struggled to give him one.

"I need to talk to you."

Alex looks up from the tablet in his hands and places it on the bed next to him. The swelling from the gash on his head has subsided, but he will have a scar near his hairline.

"What do you need?"

"Why did you pay me to dance for you when you had already paid the money I was trying to earn in the first place?"

"Because I wanted to. Because I didn't want you to worry about money. I also wanted to give Maxim what he wanted. He wanted to go to that school and I wanted to be the one to give it to him."

"Then why ask me to dance for you?"

"Because I wanted that too. I wanted to be the one you danced for, not a group of strangers. Me."

I shake my head. "What else do you want, eh? To get on my knees when you want to get off and serve you food until you get better. So that you can ignore me and tell me you can't be what I want."

"That was before."

"Oh, so now that my son is your kid, things change? I'm suddenly worthy to be by your side? Well, you know what, that's not gonna happen, *ese*."

"Be careful, Alina. I've been patient with you. You don't want to see my ugly side. You will be here with me. It is for your safety. You don't realize the magnitude of what that piece of shit has done." He clenches his teeth and his voice is dripping in anger. "Everyone knows you are the mother of an heir of the Cortez Cartel. There are pictures he took of you, Alina. He passed them around. The mother of my son has been used, beaten, and exploited. Men have pictures of what is mine. Do you know what that does to me, huh? As a man, I look weak and I failed you, Alina. So, please. Don't make feel any less for paying for something like my son's tuition and your school. Don't insult me."

"That wasn't my intention. My intention was to—"

He cuts me off. "Never to tell me about him. To raise him without me?"

He's angry but there is only one way where this is going, for me to find a way for him to let me go. I could handle his rejection but I can't handle his hate toward me. Not after everything I have gone through.

"No, that wasn't my intention either, neither was being hit, or being ridiculed or threatened. I lived in fear for the past six years. I was never loved or cared for. You were too busy falling in love with someone else." Rage boils in my veins, causing the tears spill. "Trust me, there is nothing you can do to me that hasn't been done to me already. So go ahead, *pinche pendejo*. Do you worst."

I turn away.

"Come back here, Alina. Don't make me get up—"

I walk to the kitchen and grab a Modelo from the fridge.

There are cutlery and gadgets in each of the drawers. Things I have never seen in my life. I don't drink, but I don't know what to do. I need to take the edge off at how angry and hurt I feel right now.

I try to open the beer with my hands. I'm not an expert on drinking beer obviously because the cap is glued on and won't open, causing my hand to sting.

"Look at me, Alina," Alex says behind me.

I look at him with the beer bottle in my hand. "What?"

"Give me the beer. You don't drink."

I hand him the bottle and dry my eyes with my arm the best I can. I hate crying. I feel helpless and it feels like every time I do cry, it's because of the man in front of me.

He inspects the bottle and walks over to the opposite side of the kitchen and opens a small drawer with a bottle opener and opens it taking a pull. Really?

He winces slightly, and I know he must be hurting. "You shouldn't drink while taking the pain meds," I state.

He smiles. "I'll live. I've done worse." He places the beer down on the counter. "What did I tell you about crying?" I avert my face, but he walks toward me. "You're lucky I'm banged up, *muneca*. Because I would sit you up on this counter and show you how I can make you smile."

My eyes meet his, and I feel the back of his hand on my cheek. "I promised my son I wouldn't make you cry. I promised myself to show you how much I love you any way I could. I can't say the words right now because if I did, you would doubt them. I'm asking you to find it in your heart to give me a chance."

Another man asked me the same thing and I said yes without giving him the opportunity. A man that found me amazing and said I was beautiful. He asked me what my favorite color was and bought me flowers for my first date. Something I have never experienced and it felt nice.

"What's my favorite color?" I ask.

He smirks. "Don't compare me. It's red." My chest is tight with each sob that comes, but he continues, "You want me to fight for you? I will, and I won't stop, Alina. I'll never stop until I get you, and when I do, I'm never letting you go."

Thirty-Five

ALEX

It's been two weeks and I can finally get out of my apartment without struggling. Maxim starts school, and I need to make sure Alina has financial stability and a better car. I appreciate Julio helping her and I can't get angry with him, but my relationship with Alina right now is like a chain that has been pulled and I'm being flushed down the fucking toilet.

"Where are we going?" Hector asks.

"To the car dealership."

"You're buying another car?" Carlito asks.

I take a deep breath and I know I need to rest at least for another week. It still hurts when I breathe but Maxim starts school and Alina wants to take him and pick him up every day.

She still cooks for me every day. She cleans up after herself and refuses to wear or use anything I bought her.

I thank her every day. I tell her she's beautiful even if she doesn't believe me. I watch her sleep and kiss her on her head when doesn't realize it. There are times she whispers in her sleep. She says my name, and I caress her hair, praying she gives me a chance. A chance I never knew I had the whole time she waited for me.

"Yeah."

"Is it a classic?" Julio asks.

I know he stills texts her to ask how she is doing. I'm jealous but I will look like an asshole if I tell her to ignore him. She sleeps in my bed every night and our son asleep in the next room is all that matters.

Hector pulls the G-Wagon into the car dealership where one of Leo's guys handles our cars that are sold to the immediate cartel families. It is where all the Kings get the cars for their women, and in my case, for the woman that means the most to me right now. She's my family if she doesn't know it yet.

"The King of the streets is here. What's up, *holmes*? It's ready and it is dope as fuck, " Lenny says with laughter in his eyes. I smile and nudge my chin to greet him.

Wanting to get what I came for to surprise Alina, I reply, "What's up, *ese*. Show me."

Lenny is a cool kid but he's better in selling us cars than actually running with us.

He walks us in and stops in front of the car I came for. The one I specifically ordered when she didn't notice me on the phone.

I hear Carlito whistle behind me when we stop at the shiny late model blacked out Escalade ESV.

"Damn, fool. You into Cadillacs now?" Hector asks.

Lenny steps forward and begins to open the doors and the back to show me that it is bulletproof.

"It's bulletproof. Satellite TV, PlayStation, Xbox, all the apps are loaded and the GPS installed. Run flats just in case," Lenny says, pointing at the tires.

"Good."

"Open the hood, Lenny. I need to see the engine."

"Right, right."

He opens the hood, and Julio takes a look. Our eyes meet, and I look away, trying to hold the jealousy bubbling to the surface. My eyes focus on a red car in the corner, and I smile to myself.

"What are you thinking, *cabron*," Hector says softly.

I grin. "I'm thinking my girl likes red."

He chuckles and whistles. "Yo, Lenny. *Este tambien, cabron.*"

He runs over because the kid just made what he would make in commission for three months in one night. "Yeah?"

"This one too."

"You into red, *ese*?" he asks.

"Nah, but my girl's favorite color is red."

Thirty-Six

ALINA

Khalani, Lucy, Linda, and Katalia walk in after I let them in the front door.

"Are you ready?" Linda asks.

"Auntie Lucy, look." Maxim turns in slow motion in his new uniform excitedly.

"You're so handsome, Maxim," Lucy praises him.

I smile. He looks adorable in his uniform and shoes she got him.

"You guys are spoiling him."

Lucy bats her lashes. "It's my thing."

Linda and Khalani follow me into the bedroom and go snooping in my closet. "You have got to be kidding me," Khalani yells, popping her head out. "You haven't worn any of this stuff?"

I shake my head.

"Why not?" Linda asks, looking at all the things Alex keeps buying me.

"I'm not used to it," I say quietly.

Linda nods. "I get it. That asshole fucked with your head, didn't he?"

"Can I show you something?" I ask.

I took pictures of the pictures off Danny's phone when he left it unlocked and kept the videos he actually sent me of the different women they would ransom for money when Danny would threaten me. I've never shown anyone because I knew no one could help me. Until now.

"Show me what?" Linda asks.

Lucy walks in when Maxim goes into his room to change out of his uniform. "Show us what?" she asks.

I pull up the photos he took of me and the videos of all the women that would end up dead after he would tape them pleading for their life. I even took pictures of my bruised face and body with the dates.

"This is what I had to do endure to survive. What I feared would happen to me if Danny went too far. The things he did to me are secrets I have to keep and things I could never tell anyone." I watch has Linda swipes through the phone and tears slide down her face. Lucy walks up behind her and Katalia closes her eyes, turning her face away.

Khalani looks up and her eyes meet mine. "Has Alex seen this?"

I shake my head, biting my lip. "Sometimes, I think if I didn't get pregnant, I would be better off but then I wouldn't have Maxim. I thought moving on was right thing but now I know that I can't because I'm tied to Alex through Maxim anyway, but if I didn't have him, would Alex still feel the same way about me now? Would I get fancy purses and clothes? Live in a place like this? Have his attention?"

"You can't think like that. Alex is a complicated guy but has a good heart and I've known him a long time and I've never seen him in love the way he is with you," Khalani says.

"Not even me," Lucy adds. "I don't think Alex would allow another man to touch what he considers his. He's traditional in that sense and extremely jealous."

"I agree," Linda says.

"Now let's get to the house in the east. He said to bring you there before he sends out the search party," Katalia says, dragging me out of the room but stops and grabs the designer bag Khalani was holding from my closet. "Ooh, this is nice. Valentino. This is fancy and perfect with the black jeans and cropped sweater."

I shake my head. "You couldn't resist, could you?"

"Nope." Khalani chirps handing me the bag.

⋯⋰♔⋱⋯

We get to the house in the east, and it looks like there is a huge party because all the Kings and the members are there. If feels like it was months since I last stepped into the house but it's only been two weeks. There are cars everywhere but there is one car that is covered and a huge black-out SUV that looks like a celebrity is in attendance.

I wave my hand when a cloud of smoke floats above me from the Porch. The Kings scramble to put out their joints.

"Put it out, *ese*. You know Smiley will kick your ass if Alina starts coughing. Especially, with Maxim around." I hear one of them say to the other. I don't remember all their names but I remember some of their faces.

Maxim runs inside the house. "Smiley?" he calls out.

We still haven't told him. I walk in and see some girls sitting on the couch, but my eyes narrow on one in particular. The one he fucked while I was in the other room. Why is she here?

She smirks, and my eyes dart around the room, looking for Alex. A burning sensation flows in the pit of my stomach.

"What the fuck are you looking at, *pendeja*?" Katalia is the first to check her ass.

Camila shrugs. "I was just wondering if she liked the way I taste since I fucked Smiley while she was in the next room."

I see red. I snatch her ass up off the couch and punch on her nose. Blood splatters everywhere.

"Oh, shit!" Julio comes up behind me to get me to stop punching her, but I throw him off.

I hit over and over until her face is busted up.

Alex comes up and grabs me off her. *"Princessa."* He chuckles, his lips pressing kisses on my head above my ear. "She's crying and bloody. You're going to kill her."

My chest is heaving from the adrenaline rush brought on by rage.

"She broke my nose!" Camila wails. "Do something."

Lucy goes up to her and says menacingly, "You just insulted one of the Cortez cartel's women and you expect her man to save you? You practically asked her how you tasted when you fucked her man. We should just kill you, *pinche pendeja*, and let the coyotes find you since you like to spread your legs and boast about it. *Eh, cabrona?*"

"No please," she pleads, trying to stop the blood from running down her nose.

"Get her out of here. If you come here or disrespect what is mine, I'll kill you. I warned you to stay away," Alex says quietly.

Aiden walks in and claps. "Damn, was that Lucy?"

"Nah, it was Alina," Hector says.

"You talk shit, get hit," Aiden says, and then his face goes serious. Lethal. "Next time, kill her. Now she knows."

"Come to the bedroom," Alex whispers in my ear.

I follow him to his room, and I'm surprised he has a bag packed. He closes the door and comes up behind me, pushing me gently toward the mattress. When I'm facing him, he starts to unbutton my jeans and I can tell he's struggling, probably still uncomfortable from his rib, so I help him pull them down my thighs.

He unzips his sweater and his chest ripples. I can't see if there is any bruising by his ribs, but it's darker and fading toward the center of his stomach. He taps on my inner thighs so I open them.

"Spread your legs for me, Alina. I want to taste you," he says in a raspy voice and drops to his knees. He pulls me toward the edge and nuzzles his face between my legs. "Hmm," he groans when he sucks on my clit. "I love your smell."

My eyes roll back, and I fist the sheets, experiencing for the first time someone eating me out. His tongue swipes up and down and then twirls, driving me insane.

"Fuck, Alex." I grip his hair and pull.

He increases the pressure, fucking me with his tongue, and I grind shamelessly on his face. "Oh, yes."

He swirls his tongue in a circular motion the pleasure surging between legs.

My legs begin to shake when I reach my orgasm. He grips my thighs with his hands and fucks me faster with his tongue until my vision blurs from the powerful orgasm that rips through me.

"Yes, Alex. Oh, God."

When I finally come down, he licks me clean, then kisses my pussy softly. "Your pussy taste so good." He kisses the soft skin on my inner thighs. "I can sit here and eat you out forever. You're mine, Alina."

Am I?

Thirty-Seven

ALEX

It's Friday, and I feel way better. I'm back to my old self, except I have a scar on my head that fucks up with my tapeline, but it's nothing compared to what Alina has gone through. I will make the fucker pay my way.

The front door opens, with Alina scolding Maxim. He's had his first week at school. He's so good at waking up and getting ready in the morning, but the way she's stomping through the house has me frowning.

"Why, Maxim, huh? You can't do that!"

What the fuck is going on?

She slams the kitchen drawers. "I'm sorry, Mom. That boy was picking on me."

"Look up," she demands. "Why, huh?" Emotions has her voice choked up.

I rush over and see Maxim sitting in front of her on the counter, and she's trying to rub something off his neck with water. "What's wrong?"

She turns her head. Her eyes are blotchy. She's upset, but when I look at Maxim, he's frowning, trying to dry Alina's tears, and it breaks my heart. He's adorable and I love that he's mine.

"What's wrong?"

Alina hiccups. "The school called and said Maxim got into a fight at school, and gang violence is not tolerated." She points to his neck. "Look!"

There's black bold lettering like a tattoo, but it was drawn with a marker that reads King in a child's handwriting. I cover my mouth to stifle a grin.

"Smiley has one and he's not in trouble," Maxim tries to defend himself.

"You think this is funny?" she scolds me.

"It will come off, Alina," I say with a grin.

"Yeah, it comes off but not what he said to the kids and to the staff at the school. He said he's going to kick anyone's ass who messes with him because he runs with the East Hillside Kings. They threatened to expel him from the school."

I whip my head in her direction, and my eye twitches in anger. "Oh yeah, who said that?"

"The principal. Mr. Martin."

"Come on."

"What?"

"Get Maxim." I grab my keys. "We're going to the school."

After the twenty-five-minute drive to the school, I look at Maxim in the rearview mirror and he keeps biting his nails. I remember when I was a kid, I used to do the same thing when my mother was upset with me. Maxim may be the spitting image of Alina, but he acts like me. I admit I was a Momma's boy, and I turned ruthless when she passed. I was angry because she was gone, and I had no control.

I know Maxim cares more about upsetting his mother than the situation at school, but Mr. Martin needs to understand who Maxim is and who his father his. Better yet, who his mother is.

When we arrive, we are shown into the principal's office. There are three chairs in front of the wood desk, and there are frames that hold prestigious awards the school has received for academic excellence. This is the last place they will look to hurt our kids. Bodyguards and chauffeurs are a norm in this type of setting.

"Welcome, Miss. Flores, I usually don't see anyone without an appointment, but this is a serious matter. One that will not be tolerated. I have allowed the opportunity for you to educate him on how to properly conduct himself in this school."

I clear my throat and pull the hoodie of my head so he can see I have a similar tattoo on my neck. His eyes widen, but he quickly composes himself.

"Do you know who I am?" I ask. "Does the name Cortez mean anything to you? Montgomery, Sincere, Galiano, or Santos. Do those last names ring a bell?"

He loosens his tie nervously and swallows. "I-I believe that I do. And who are you?"

"I'm Maxim's father, and if my son kicks another boy's ass, you look the other way. If my son doodles King wherever he wants, you look the other way." I sit up and lower my voice in a warning tone. "If you threaten to expel my son, I will come here and deal with you myself." I lean close to Maxim say, "Wait outside for one second." He does as he is told, and when the door closes, my smile turns lethal. "The only thing left will be your fingernails and your teeth that I will bury with the collection I have. Miss Flores is really Mrs. Cortez. Make sure you let that sink in."

"I-I'm sorry, " he stammers. "My sincerest apologies. I didn't know. What do I say to the other boy's parents?"

I snicker and shrug. "Tell them you did it."

"But that would–"

"You should have looked the other way and said nothing. You remember that next time."

…•❦…

"Are you really my dad?" Maxim asks from the back seat of the Escalade with a hopeful expression.

I glance toward Alina, and she nods telling me that I should tell him the truth.

"Yeah. I'm your father, Maxim."

"Is Mommy your wife?"

I take a deep breath and grip the steering wheel because I want her to be. Desperately.

"No, Maxim. Mommy isn't married," she replies.

"Why?"

"Because your mommy and daddy aren't together in that way."

He tilts his head. "Are you married to the bad man?"

"No," I say. "She isn't married to the bad man. I will protect you both from now on, Maxim. I promise."

I'm not going to allow Maxim to blame Alina for not telling me. She had a reason, and I hope she doesn't think I resent her for it because I don't.

"Am I still in trouble?'

I place my hand over Alina's, silently telling her to let me handle it.

"Not this time, but you can't go around hitting people all the time."

He lowers his head in defeat. "Okay. I'm sorry."

"Did he deserve it?"

He looks up and nods. "Yep. He was mean and said I didn't have a dad and that his dad was going to be my dad because he said my mommy has a big butt."

Alina cringes.

"Oh, yeah. What was his name?" I ask.

"Jeremy Johansen."

I guess Jeremy's dad is going to get his ass kicked too.

Thirty-Eight

ALINA

I'm stepping out of the shower after Lucy picked up Maxim to take him to the zoo with Katalia, Niko, and Katalia's little brother. She's been great, and she assured me that there is nothing between her and Alex. She wants to see us both happy, but I'm still scared. What if Alex changes his mind. His father's words echo in my mind. Wife or whore. If I decide to be his wife, then will that mean he will have mistresses?

The bathroom door opens, and Alex walks in, wearing sweatpants. The outline of his cock is clearly visible. My clit throbs, but I'm too shy to make a move or give him a hint that I want him to touch me. I don't want to seem desperate. I want a man to want me because he finds me attractive, and with Alex, it's complicated.

The night he went down on me was his way of reassuring me that there was nothing more going on between him and Camila, but it wasn't love.

"Come here," he demands.

I walk over, and he pulls the towel from my hands. My hair is towel dried and my skin is flushed from the hot shower.

"Is everything alright?"

He stands behind me and kisses my neck. I watch our reflection in the vanity mirror. His bare chest feels cool on my back.

"Bend over and place your hands on the counter." I do as he asks. He grips my waist hearing the sound of his pants dropping to the floor and feel the tip of his cock at my entrance. "Open your eyes, Alina."

My eyes open, and I see his bottom lip in his mouth and feel the sharp sting when he rams his cock inside me, jolting me forward. I moan loud at how full and good he feels stretching inside me.

"Keep your eyes open." He spreads his hands over the cheeks of my ass. "Damn, baby. You have a nice ass. Fuck."

He rams into me faster and faster. It's raw, hard, and all Alex.

My thighs are sticky and wet. My tits bounce with each thrust. He grips my hair with one hand and my ass with the other, fucking me savagely.

My walls clench around his cock when I'm on the brink of coming. It's been so long since I've come like this. The only time was the first time with Alex. Then all the other times I couldn't because of Danny. The way he would treat me. The way I would cringe every time he would touched me.

"Hey." Alex's voice breaks me out of my stupor. "Where did you go? I asked if you were okay."

"Nowhere," I respond, but the look in my eyes must tell him differently because he stops. I pull away from him and his cock slips out of me. I find it funny that all this time I wished for this moment, I never thought my mind would remind me of all the times someone used me because of him. Danny knew what he was doing; he was making sure Alex had what was left. Someone broken and damaged. "I'm s-sorry," I stammer. I back away and walk into the shower. "I can't."

Water pours on my head as I slide down the tiles feeling ashamed and embarrassed. I don't know what is wrong with me, but my head is all over the place.

I wipe the water from my eyes, thinking Alex is going to come in the shower, but he doesn't. He walks away and closes the door.

He leaves me.

Just like Danny said he would. Because I'm not good enough.

Thirty-Nine

ALEX

I take a pull from my beer and take in the city below through the glass windows. Any minute, Linda will walk in with Maxim. She's taken the part of being an aunt seriously. She feels that so much time was lost but while that is true, there is also the problem of Alina and me.

What happened in the bathroom was something that has never happened to me with anyone. She zoned out, lost in the recesses of her mind. I called her name and was about to come; I wanted her to get off first, but she was blankly staring into the mirror. She wasn't enjoying it——enjoying me the way I was enjoying her.

The door opens and Maxim comes running toward me with souvenirs and hats with zoo animals all over it. "S—Dad. Look!" he says, full of laughter and excitement. He holds up a bag of different animal toys.

"That is awesome."

"Tia got me all this stufff. I saw all the animals, but some of them stink."

I chuckle and address Linda, "You're spoiling him."

"And?"

"And, when you have your kid, don't get mad when I do it."

She grins, then pries, "What's wrong?"

Linda is not going to let it slide. She knows something is eating me up inside. Alina hasn't come out, and I don't know what to do. I'm used to having women come to me, and if I feel like fucking, I do and that's it. No strings. No attachments, and if they want more, I remind them of my rules.

The problem is that now I'm interested. I'm in love with her and I don't know want to do about it.

Linda asks Maxim to go to his room and wash up, then joins me on the couch. "Where's Alina?"

I gaze at the skyline and take another pull from my beer. "In the shower."

"What happened?"

I tell her everything because I'm desperate and I don't have the balls to tell any of the guys that the girl I love is not into me sexually. She cooks, sleeps, and takes care of our son. Every day since we moved here, she sits with Maxim and helps him with homework on school nights and tends to me. I thought the other night I went down on her; we were moving in the right direction.

"So, you left her in the shower on her own? You didn't talk to her? Ask her if she was okay, Alex?"

I didn't do any of that.

I was coward and I was scared she'd reject me.

Linda sighs and pulls out her phone and begins to scroll through it. "She's going to kill me when she finds out I sent myself these from her old phone when she showed us, but I think you should see it for yourself. Maybe, you'll understand what she's going through and has been through. Even if she didn't want him, Alex, she was still a victim of abuse. That kind of thing breaks you and I think her pain is the worst because she had to watch the man that she did love leave her." My phone dings. "Trust me, Alex, she paid a heavy price to save you and your son, even knowing you didn't reciprocate her feelings for you."

I get up from the couch, knowing I can't watch whatever she gave me here. It needs to be in private.

"Stay here and settle Maxim in for me. Alina is in the shower, and I don't want to leave Maxim out here alone."

The elevator opens to Linda and Colton's penthouse, and I'm not surprised to find Leo, Aiden, and Mase.

"What's up, primo," Mase greets me.

I turn to Colton. "I need your computer to play a file Linda sent me."

"Send it to me."

"Joaquin is coming. He isn't happy," Mase says.

Joaquin is the least of my worries. He can get over it later. Alina is mine and nothing else matters. Just her and Maxim.

"It's up," Colton says, getting up from the desk.

I make my way over and start browsing.

I keep looking through the file, checking out photographs and videos. My vision blurs. A lump forms in my throat. A wail pierces through the air. When Mase comes up behind me, I realize it's me who's making the sound.

I'm being dragged away, but I can unsee what I saw. The pictures of Alina. The videos of those women.

Mase tries to calm me down, but I want to get to her. I want to tell how sorry I am. I need to see her. I need to love her.

"Relax, Alex," Mase says, hugging me. "We're looking. We will find him and you will make him pay."

"You need to be with her," Aiden says. "Show her that it wasn't for nothing. Show her that you understand. Show her she's your queen. *La reina* of everything you run."

"We have all been there, *ese*. We have all gone through our own shit. Don't let him destroy your family," Colton chimes in.

Leo walks up to me and lowers his voice. "Don't let him destroy you. This is what he wants. We are all family and nothing breaks us."

I wipe my face and try to swallow, but my throat burns from screaming. "Let me know when you get him to the warehouse. And make sure he's alive."

Forty

ALEX

lina is in the bathroom, probably getting ready to make breakfast. Last night, I waited until she fell asleep to come in the bedroom. I needed to clear my head and silently cry in the living room. It wasn't just the pictures of her naked or the videos of those women. The sick fuck took pictures of her face when he would beat her. I saw what he did to her.

Then the anger set in and I made a checklist in my head of all the ways I can torture and kill that bastard to bring the most pain

After that, I went to sleep, and now here I am, trying to figure out my next move when it comes to the mother of my beautiful son. I look over and see her bag on the nightstand happy that she chose to use one that I bought for her. I like that one too.

I find a wallet and the key to both cars and the apartment. What gets my attention is an aluminum packet with pills. Birth control.

I take them out, placing the bag back where I found it, and head to the kitchen to discard them.

I check on Maxim, and he's still asleep so I walk back in toward the bathroom. I don't bother to knock and barge right in, heading to the sink to brush my teeth like we've been doing this for years.

Alina watches me from her side of the sink while applying moisturizer on her face. Her skin is all clean and glowing. I can smell her soap and floral perfume even with the toothpaste in my mouth. I rinse but keep watching her from the corner of my eye.

Her legs are toned. The globes of her ass are firm when she moves around, and I notice her tank top is thin. I can see the outline of her nipples. I turn to the side, not ashamed that my dick is hard as a rock from looking at her.

Her hands stop when she notices my hard cock. Her tongue peeks out, and I do what she doesn't expect me to do. I walk up to her and wipe her hands with a towel, and she lets me.

I pull her to the bedroom and make sure I lock the door and turn on the TV so I can watch Maxim from the camera.

"What–"

My mouth crashes against hers. She whimpers when my tongue meets hers in a swirl of mint and hot breaths. I pick her up and lay her on the bed.

I kiss her neck, trailing soft kisses down to her breasts. "I love you," I rasp.

I gave her up once, but I'm not doing it again. I'm going to fight for her. Wait for her. Even if it takes an eternity.

She kisses me back and runs her hands behind my back. I settle between her legs, but all I do is pepper kisses on her lips, her breast, and her face. But I hold back.

Baby steps.

Forty-One

ALINA

We've established a routine now. He wakes up when I do, and he caresses me. He kisses me and says that he loves me. Is it pity? I'm not sure. Is that how he really feels? I don't know. Maybe he thinks he needs to feel that way.

I just know that if it weren't because of Maxim and Joker, he wouldn't love me. And that stings. Because I know I wouldn't be here if none of it happened.

"What are you thinking about?"

I look at Julio when he walks in his office at the shop and say, "Nothing."

He closes the door and sits in the chair by the wall, overlooking the bay at his shop.

I know I shouldn't be here talking to him, but every day after I take Maxim to school, I stop by and we talk. Sometimes I just sit here listening to the sounds of cars being restored.

"What's wrong?"

"Nothing, I just feel...confused."

"It's normal to feel like that. I'm surprised you don't need therapy for what that asshole did to you. Also, why say nothing is bothering you when something is eating you inside and someone is trying to help you?"

"You first," I hedge.

"I like to feel that I run something and I'm tired of getting dirty. Day in and day out. I like to make the car better than it was but to do that, I have to step back and visualize it coming together. If I'm dirty and under the hood, I can't do that."

"That makes sense."

"Now, it's your turn."

"I'm used to it. Dealing with the bad things on my own. Surviving without anyone's help because in the end, I have to be strong or I fail. I die. I let people down. There is no use in saying anything when people don't take the time to pay attention."

"But I asked you if you were okay and you said nothing."

"Because it's too late. It's done. Like stage four cancer. Survival rate is low. It's up to the person to fight or an act of God to survive. Sometimes, it's better to say nothing and let things be. Accept the crumbs you do get."

"What do you think has a low rate of surviving?"

Julio watches me, but I think he understands my silence. "You and Smiley. You think it's a lost cause. Why?"

I twirl the strands of my long hair, threading it through my fingers, and ask, "If you loved someone, or better yet, someone like me, and had the intention of falling in love after I gave myself to you, would you leave me? Would you sleep with someone else right after? Could you fall in love with someone else?"

He looks away briefly and then his gaze lands on me when he says softly, "Not for a second. But he didn't know. He was young."

He still doesn't get it. The turmoil that is my mind right now. I tried to keep Maxim a secret to keep him safe and survive Danny's threats for so long that I lost myself. I was so hung up on loving Alex that I forgot to ask myself if I had the chance to escape it all and meet him again, could he love me? Would he feel something for me? It only changed when he found out that Maxim was his.

"Before he found out that all this time Maxim was his. Is he still too young? Or did he feel the same? Because if I can recall, he wasn't trying to stick his cock in me, telling me he loved me. He didn't care when he was screwing that pendeja in his room and I had to listen. I had to hear him tell me it was all in the past and that he couldn't be what I wanted. So, which is it?"

"I'm sorry, Alina. But I understand."

I feel bad dumping my problems on him and I never thanked him for being a gentleman. For being nice to me and genuine.

"I forgot to say thank you."

"For what?"

"For being the first man besides my son to tell me I was beautiful. I'm sure you have said it before, and it doesn't mean much to some, but to me, it did."

He slides his hand over his face and sighs. "Fuck, Alina. Do you have to make this so hard?"

I look away, confused. "I don't understand what you mean. I'm sorr–"

"I'm in love with you, Alina. Ever since I saw you the first time dancing at the club. I know that is not what you need right now with everything going on but I'm trying to accept you can never be mine because Alex will kill me. All I can do is be here for you because you deserve that. You deserve so much, *Princessa*."

Shit.

"I didn't mean to hurt you."

"You didn't. You can still come here if you want. I love it when you come and talk to me. If you want to help in the office. I can pay you. It will give you something to do until you start school."

I look around the dusty office filled with papers and smile. "Are you giving me a job?"

He steps back and slides his hands in his pockets. "Why yes, I am. Four hours a day, five days a week. Lunch included. No work on school holidays. Those days are for Maxim."

"I'll take it."

He nods and gives me a smile. "*Orale*. See you tomorrow and don't be late."

Forty-Two

ALEX

Four more days, and every day, I don't miss a morning that I don't kiss her and caress her skin. I bathe with her in the shower. I help her with Maxim in the morning, but she leaves and doesn't come back until after lunch. She's never hungry, but I still have food for her anyway. I know she goes somewhere, but I don't ask and I don't check.

I don't want her to feel that I'm smothering her. I don't want to push her sexually because of what happened last time.

Tonight, I have planned a movie night like when we were teenagers and she would fall asleep in my arms. I'm not sure what to watch because of Maxim but I don't care. We can watch Mary Poppins, for all I care. He can choose.

I scroll through the movies, selecting all the appropriate ones by ratings so I don't corrupt my son before he's old enough. I check my phone and Alina should be getting here any minute with Maxim from school.

The door opens, and the sound of Maxim's little feet warms my heart.

"Hi, dad," he beams.

"Como esta, hijo."

"I'm starving," he says dramatically.

"I'm going to go get him washed up and start dinner," she says.

"That's okay. Go ahead and help Maxim out. I already have dinner. I thought it would be good to have a movie night."

She smirks. "A movie night?"

"Yeah, I made food and everything. I bought popcorn and candy too."

She looks over at the couch where I have blankets and pillows like a fourteen year old, excited for his first sleepover.

I pause when I notice dust on her jeans but I don't say anything. "Okay."

. . .\\⨊//. . .

We're settled on the couch after I made menudo soup. It's a Mexican dish I learned how to make when my mother was sick, and it was her last few months before she died of cancer. I stayed with her in the daytime and Linda would stay with her in the nighttime so I can make money doing runs for the Kings.

"The food was good. Thank you," she says, placing the spoon in the bowl.

"My pleasure."

We finally settle on The Incredibles. One of Maxim's favorites so I add it to my favorites list and all the ones he couldn't decide so he could watch them whenever he wants.

When the movie starts, Alina doesn't sit close to me like I'm used to and I start to get nervous because she's still distant with me. I don't see the want in her eyes that I recognized a little too late but I'm trying. After Maxim falls asleep and I tuck him his bed, she leans close when I sit back down.

I pick up the remote, and I scroll to the adult section. "What would you like to watch?"

She leans her head back and my arm is sprawled behind the back of the couch. "Whatever you want to watch."

"Do you still watch the scary stuff?"

She snorts. "Oh God, no. Try watching the Chainsaw Massacre with a child. You'll scar him for life. Not even when I was pregnant with Maxim. I read somewhere that babies feel things in the womb."

"Oh, that makes sense. So, what did you watch?"

"Meditation videos, romcom movies, and I even read romance novels."

"The dirty ones or the sweet ones that are far-fetched."

"What do you mean far-fetched?"

"*No, manches*. Do you think that stuff really happens? All the men are ripped and buff and good-looking. They are all players that have good looks and they fall for this one woman and live happily ever after like they don't have bills. People don't even talk like that."

She laughs. "You're ripped and have muscles. And you're a player."

"You're right," I deadpan.

She blinks.

Then she shoves me playfully, and I laugh. "You're so full of yourself."

I raise my hands in mock surrender. "Hey, I'm just agreeing with you. Those are your words but you're right. I have fallen for this one woman and I'm trying to live happily ever after."

Her smile drops, and her eyes meet mine. I inch closer, and the soft skin of her lips brushes against mine. Smooth and soft. My tongue slides out and swipes the seam of her lips.

Lightning flashes across the city skyline as rain pelts the windows. My hands cup her face, and I kiss her.

I pull her toward me so I can deepen the kiss. Her hands slide up under my shirt, and I've never wanted someone to touch me so much in my entire life. There is nothing like the feeling of her hands on my skin. The fullness of her lips and the look of wonder in her eyes when I remain still, letting her do what she wants. How she wants it.

The rain keeps coming down in sheets against the glass, the lightning flashing in the distance, but there is no sound of thunder.

It catches her attention, and I pull the blanket away and tug her so she can follow me toward the sliding glass door.

Her eyes find mine and a look of confusion crosses her features when she sees me undo the safety latch and open the door that leads to the balcony.

"Follow me."

I stand behind her and let the spray of water hit our skin. It's cold and I can hear her intake of breath as the water plasters against her skin. Our clothes are drenched and our hair's soaked. The thing keeping us warm is each other.

My lips press against the side of her neck, followed by my tongue tasting the cold water mixed with the taste of her.

I grow hard behind her, and I pull her close by her hips so she can feel it. My finger slides under the band of her pajama shorts.

When I reach her clit, her body sags against mine, and her neck arches. I nibble, bite, and kiss her shoulder, rubbing her clit in a rhythm while the rain cools the heat we're creating.

"Alex..."

"I'm right here. Always, *muneca*. I'm...right here."

"Someone is watching us."

My head snaps up, and across the building from this one, there is a man standing in his apartment. I know there are rich executives that live on this street. I guess he is trying to see how far we'd go. How far we'd take it.

My nose caresses her wet skin. "Then let's give him a show."

Her chest rises and falls, and I turn her to face me, removing her top and bottom, and she helps me remove my sweats until we're both naked.

I lift her up, wrapping her legs around my waist. I hold her steady so I can slide the tip of my cock insider her wet heat. The man is now watching us with a pair of binoculars. I've never been into voyeurism, but with Alina, I want to push the limit without allowing anyone to touch her. I want to explore things with her. Make memories with her. Love her.

I hold her in an angle with her back toward the man watching and I slowly inch inside her while our eyes are locked. We both struggle not to blink while the drops of water slide down our skin.

She gasps when I'm fully seated inside her, letting her adjust to my size.

"More," she says.

My eyes flick up to her. "Scream for me."

She fucking screams for me as I take her hard under the rain. Her tits bounce with each thrust. Her legs grip my waist tight, while she holds herself up like I'm the pole she dances with.

Fuck, she's amazing. Her pussy is amazing, and fuck me, I'm not going to last.

"Alex, I'm coming. I'm coming!" I don't let up until her orgasm crashes around her.

Her legs slowly slide down my hips, and I turn her around and hold her head steady by her hair so she can see the man watching me fuck her. My lips ghost her ear, and I say softly right before entering her, "Let him watch."

I slide into her, and I fuck her while she holds the concrete part of the railing until I'm emptying inside her with a roar escaping my throat. After we both come down, I hold her body from going limp.

"I've never done that before."

"Me neither. But that's what makes it so special, Alina, because it's us This is...us."

Forty-Three

ALINA

I snap out of the floating feeling that is going through me after the most intense orgasm I have ever had. My legs and pussy are sore from last night.

Alex carried me to the bathroom and bathed me. When he placed me naked on the bed, wrapped in a fluffy robe, I closed my eyes, and the next moment, Maxim was jumping on the bed, already ready for me to take him to school.

Alex made him breakfast and got him ready. He offered to take him, but I needed to go to work.

"Are you okay?"

I lift my head from the stack of invoices I was organizing. "Huh?"

Julio walks over and leans against the desk with a darker shade of Dickie pants and his black bandana hanging from his pocket. "You look—"

"What?" I ask with a raised brow.

He rubs the stubble on his chin. "I don't mean any disrespect, but you look freshly fucked."

I look away, embarrassed.

I can't stop thinking about last night. Alex fucking me in the rain with an audience. I felt free and sexy. It was hot. He was hot with the water hitting his tattooed skin.

"Is that what you see?"

"Yeah, I see that you liked whatever happened and I'm happy for you."

"Are you truly?"

"I'm happy if you're happy because I love you, Alina. I want you to be happy, and if he makes you happy, then I would do anything to help you be happy even if that means it's not with me."

"You see, that right there, *ese.* That is what I'm talking about. How the hell aren't you married or have a serious girlfriend or something. A ride or die."

He leans forward on the desk and smiles. "Because I never knew a woman like you existed."

Fuck me. He makes it so hard not to like him.

"Lunch is coming, " he says.

"You don't have to do that. I can buy my own lunch, you know."

"Not with me. I don't care how much money he gives you. Now, tell me how's Maxim doing in the new school."

I told him what happened to Maxim and how Alex went over there and threatened the principal to look the other way or he would erase him from the planet.

"He's empowered."

Julio chuckles. "I would have done the same."

"So, you agree with Alex?"

He nods. "You had a kid from a man that knows both worlds. He's a gangster first before he's a cartel king, Alina. What do you think would happen? Maxim is his love child. There is nothing that little boy could do that would be wrong in Alex's eyes."

"That's what I'm afraid of. He's creating the next generation of a monster."

"Someone has to be the monster, Alina. You just thought you were being abused by one, but the truth is, that bastard did that because he's the coward. The monster is the one that can save you from the darkness of your hell. Nothing is going to help that piece of shit when he finds him, Alex's street name may be Smiley, but people haven't seen the true evil of that smile. I saw it the day he pulled the trigger because a man thought you were something that you're not. It was like a switch, Alina. You're the switch that unleashes the evil that lives inside Alex."

His father said the same thing.

"What do you mean?"

I get that Alex isn't the boy next door or anything like that--he's a product of his environment. An environment he chose to be a part of.

Julio glances down for a second, and when he looks up, his expression is honest and his eyes are sincere. "I've never seen him look at a woman the way he looks at you. You are the love of his life, Alina, and Maxim is the result of that love. That *vato* will set fire, destroy anything, and anyone for you. The night I picked you up and you walked out to go out with me, that broke him. He didn't know that Maxim was his and he may have left you all those years ago, but maybe he thought he wasn't good enough for you and felt he had to let you go. He's not going to walk away from you and he's not going to give you to someone else."

There is a knock on the door and our food arrives and we begin to eat.

"Why are you so good to him?"

"Because he helped me. I have all this because of him. Hector and Esperanza have a paid house because they offered to take care of your son when you got here as way of gratitude."

I didn't know that. Now I'm glad I came here if it resulted in something good.

"Is he treating you differently because of me?"

He places the plastic fork on the tray and wipes his mouth before responding with, "You mean like a jealous boyfriend? Hell, yes. He wants to kick my ass. He threatened to kill me if I touched you."

I laugh, but I know Alex means it in a good way. "Good thing I like you and won't let him."

"Gee, thanks."

⋯⫶⩘⫶⋯

After picking up Maxim, I walk into the apartment where Alex is sitting at the dining table with his laptop open.

"Hi, Dad."

Alex looks up from looking at the screen, but when he responds to Maxim, he's looking at me. "Hey, Maxim."

"I had fun in school today."

"You did?"

He gives him a hug. "Yep, I'm going to go wash my hands so I can eat. I'm hungry."

I love watching Alex with him. When Maxim goes to his room to wash up, Alex asks, "Where were you?"

I haven't told him I work four hours at Julio's shop on school days. I'm not ready to tell him because I'm afraid of his reaction and I like helping Julio out. I like our talks and he's respectful. It's my hideout from coming back and facing Alex alone.

"I took Maxim to school and picked him up."

"I get that, but where did you go while he was at school?"

"I drove around," I lie.

He scratches his brow and places his elbows on the table. "Every day?"

I play stupid like I didn't hear him while I move around in the kitchen. "Huh?"

"I said, every day."

I pause and look up with a pot in my hand, and our eyes lock. He knows I'm avoiding the question. He could track me down if he wanted, but I think he was giving me my space and I'm taking advantage of it.

He gets up and turns on the TV when Maxim comes running

down the hallway. "Maxim, watch TV for a minute. I need to talk to Mommy," Alex tells him, but he is staring at me with a straight face.

"Okay," Maxim says, sitting on the couch.

"Go to the bedroom, Alina." I bite my lip nervously and wash my hands. "Now, Alina."

Once we are in the bedroom and the door is closed, he pushes me against the door and grips my neck.

"What are you doing?"

"This will only take a minute."

He forces his hand down the front side of my jeans and hooks his finger inside my pussy, and I gasp. "What the fuck, Alex?"

He pushes two fingers inside my entrance, and I shamelessly get wet. He fingers me. He brings them to his nose, then licks them clean, making a popping sound. "Now, that we have that out of the way, where were you?"

I smile sarcastically because he thinks I'm fucking someone else. "*Estas loco.*"

"*Si, por ti.* I'm crazy for you. If I find out you're fucking someone else, I swear I'll kill him and make you watch. After I'm done, I'll fuck you right there until you understand that you're mine. Where were you, Alina?"

"None of your business."

"Alright. Fine."

He releases me, reaching around to open the door. When I move to pass him, he grabs my face and kisses me hard. I wrap my arms around his neck because fuck, he's intense. He's passionate and I want more of him. I want more of last night.

When he pulls back breathless, he says, "I missed you."

Forty-Four

ALEX

Alex

I'm a jealous prick when it comes to Alina. I'll go insane if she wants someone else and the crazy part is, I have no right. I have no right to demand anything from her, but she's the pulse that beats inside me, and without it, I'm dead because there is no life without her.

My sister waves, and I kiss my son on his forehead.

When I carefully walk back into the bedroom, I close the door to wake up my girl. I asked Linda to watch Maxim for me.

When I'm about to slide in the bed and wake her up, I notice a big book on the dresser. I take it and make my way to the living room and sit.

I open it and the first page is like taking me back in time. I see the date of birth and the time Maxim was born and where. It pains me to see he was born in a community hospital for people with no insurance.

When I turn the page, it's like a scrap book. Pictures of Alina pregnant. Her hand in each stage of her belly, but I notice one thing in all those pictures—she's alone. There's no one with her. No one to feel him kick or even take the picture. There are all selfies that she printed and stuck them on the pages of the book to save them as memories. Like a time capsule of her journey having my son while I was gone.

I look at the pregnancy test with a date on it, and I close my eyes. I was still in L.A., and around her. I ignored her glances. I even ignored her phone calls. I thought it was the best thing to not talk about what happened between us because I didn't want to hurt her, but maybe she wanted to tell me and I was already fucking around, trying to forget her while she nurtured a part of me. Kept it alive.

She could have had an abortion, but she didn't because she loved what we created so much, and I abandoned her. I keep flipping as the tears roll down my face. So perfect and beautiful, and I missed it.

Then a memory pops in my mind. The day at the pool when Lucy asked me to touch her stomach and the look of hurt that crossed her face. I get to the last page, and I see a picture of me and Maxim asleep on the couch after watching a movie.

It reads Father and Son. *Que la virgin de Guadalupe los protege para siempre.* May the Virgin of Guadalupe protect you always. I love you forever.

Forty-Five

ALINA

My eyes pop open, and I bolt up from the bed, but an arm that feels like a concrete block on my waist, prevents me from climbing out.

"It's Saturday, and Maxim is with Linda at Katalia's. Khalani and Lucy are baby shopping, again. I didn't want to wake you so I made him breakfast and got him ready."

"You're spoiling me. I'm going to end up being a lazy mother."

"Never. Anyway, I have a lot of catching up to do," he says softly.

I cover my mouth and smile, getting up to go brush my teeth. "I would love to answer you but not with my morning breath."

"It doesn't bother me."

"Yeah, until you smell it," I call out, pushing his hand away, and making my way to the bathroom.

"You're wrong!" he singsongs.

When I'm done washing my face, he comes in, and I yelp when he picks me up and tosses me on the bed.

"Alex!"

He hovers over me and the silk negligee he bought me rides up, exposing my stomach. He presses tender kisses on the lower part of my belly.

"What are you doing?"

"I'm kissing the spot where my baby came from."

Butterflies swarm in my stomach, and I watch him focusing on the tattoo of the small upside down cross under the corner of his eye, and I wonder when he got it. I caress it. "When did you get this?"

"When I killed enough. It means I'm unworthy like Peter in the bible when he requested the cross be put upside down when he was crucified. He believed he wasn't worthy to be crucified like Jesus."

"You don't think you're worthy?"

"Not for the things I've done and not for things I will have to do. I'm not a good guy, Alina."

"I think bad guys want to be good, but I don't think you're bad."

His finger caresses my belly and his tongue follows the tingles he leaves behind. "Why?"

He kisses my belly button.

"Because you gave me the most beautiful thing in this world and I'm trying to protect him from the evil that wants to hurt you."

He closes his eyes. "I don't deserve you, but I'm not letting you go. Ever."

Shit. "You're going to have to because I have an appointment."

"Where?"

"I need to refill my birth control. They're missing. I had them in my bag and now they're gone."

He looks away with a look of guilt. "I threw them out. So you don't need to go because you don't need them."

"Alex?"

He doesn't say anything, but he hooks his fingers under my panties with a gleam in his eyes and slides them down my thighs.

He aligns himself, pulling his shorts to release his cock. The metal from the tip of his cock rubs on my clit, and I open my legs wider.

"I want to have more babies with you. I want you to be my wife, my whore, the mother of my child——my everything."

He lifts my legs over his shoulders and slides inside me, turning his head and kissing my thighs.

"Alex," I whisper.

"Yeah."

"Fuck me."

I want him to take me how he wants.

I tilt my head as he spreads me open. I brace myself because the look in his eyes tells me he is not going to be gentle.

"Hold on, *Princessa*."

He angles his cock and begins to fuck me hard.

My vision clouds when he hits my G-spot. My pussy soaks his cock, and all I can hear are the wet sounds.

"Your cunt is so greedy, baby. It doesn't need my tongue, does it? It gets wet all on its own waiting for my cock. Every morning, you will leave with my cum dripping from your pussy."

Holy fuck. I feel so full, and his words are so dirty. He holds my legs and grinds into the same spot over and over, and I swear, I think he is going to dislocate my hip. He's ruthless, pumping savagely inside me.

"Fuck, this pussy is good."

I can't take it, and I come on a scream, but he doesn't stop. He pulls out while rubbing my clit with the metal in circles, teasing another one out. Then he flips me on my stomach

"Do you know how many times I wanted to fuck you?"

"How many?"

He pulls me up and scrapes his teeth on my cheek and whispers, "I'll show you."

He smacks my ass. I arch and stick my ass out, and he growls. The tip of his cock slides up and down my slit from behind. "Can I have it?"

"Yes."

"Did–" he trails off.

"No. I've never."

"It hurts until you get used to it. You don't have to if you don't want to. Maybe next time when you're ready."

"I want to see how it feels."

He slides his finger, coating it with my cum, and circling my rear hole. I feel the pressure and the sting of pain, and I wince, but it feels good at the same time. It feels different.

"Play with yourself."

I slide my hand between my legs and rub my clit. "Mm," I moan.

The pressure feels good, albeit a bit with pressure.

"What do you like, Alina?"

"I liked the night on the balcony in the rain where we were being watched. I liked that we were out in the open."

"Hmm. You liked that someone was watching us. Is that why you like dancing? You like it but hate it at the same time because it's for a different reason."

"Yes," I hiss.

He pushes his thumb deeper, and I arch, sliding my finger inside my cunt. "Alex, please."

He lifts his hand wrapping it around my neck and I arch my back.

"Fuck, baby. You're so beautiful. Perfect."

I thought wanting different things when it came to sex meant that I was fucked up or that I was sick. I wanted to feel wanted for so long and was forced to dance. But with Alex, he doesn't judge me, and when he kept saying he couldn't be what I wanted, the truth was, all I wanted to feel was what he gave me the first time —raw sex.

The kind where a man comes inside you and shows you how he claimed you as his.

I guess falling pregnant so fast and worrying about how I was going to survive didn't allow me to grow internally and know what a relationship full of love meant. I understood that I loved him but I never knew what it was to be in a relationship with him. I was left waiting and hoping he would come back and save me. Save us.

He inserts another finger, stretching my ass slowly, and I breathe through the pain. He slides his cock in my cunt, and the pressure feels so good. "Little by little, I'll stretch you until you can take me, *Princessa*."

"Yes," I hiss, laying my cheek on the mattress and spreading my ass for him.

"Like I said, greedy pussy. You like it when someone gets off watching us fuck."

I respond by pulling away and switching positions so that I'm straddling him. I lift myself, using his shoulders, and impale his cock grinding my hips.

His head leans back, his hands on my waist, and I fuck him. He sucks on my breasts, and I hold his face, watching his tongue twirl, lick, and suck.

He begins to thrust, and I bounce on his cock in a rhythm.

He holds my body close to his face, leaving hickeys in his wake. On my breasts and neck until he stills, closing his eyes. "I'm going to come and hard."

A moan escapes my lips. Our eyes lock, foreheads touch and we are both sweaty, we're fucking, and then I feel it. His cum spills inside me as I ride the wave, feeling his cock throb between my legs. "I love you," he says.

Forty-Six

ALEX

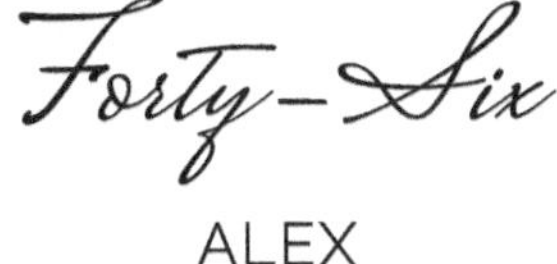

I pull up to the warehouse. I left Alina and Maxim at home asleep when I got Aiden's call that Joker is inside.

Mase is waiting by the door with a look of determination when I walk up. "Ready?" he asks.

I crack my neck. "I've been waiting a hot minute to get to this motherfucker."

The side door to the warehouse opens and Colton walks out, giving me a fist bump.

"You've been fucking nonstop. I hope you let that girl breathe. She has been holed up with you in that apartment. Are you going to let anyone play with her?"

"Fuck you, dick. You did the same with my sister. And when it comes to Alina, no touching."

"Damn," Mase teases me.

I give him a look. "I don't share my woman with anyone. I'm a greedy motherfucker when it comes to Alina. You can watch but you can't touch."

"Did you make that up? Because If I can recall, you loved to share."

"Fuck off. Now, where's Leo?"

"Inside, torturing the asshole that touched that fat culazo you have at home. You know, I wanted to ask, is her ass real?" Colton asks, and Mason bellows in laughter.

I shove Colton hard. "Stop looking at her ass."

"But you just said we could look," Colton counters.

Mase taps me on my shoulder playfully. "Is it real?"

"Yes, asswipe," I snap.

"No mames, cabron. We just want to know how you handle all that ass?" Colton adds, snickering.

Alina does have a nice ass. I know they are giving me shit now because I've been single for so long and I've never had a serious girlfriend or been this overprotective of a woman.

Mase throws open the door. "We're fucking with you. Now let's fuck this puto up."

We walk toward the back where we handle all the trash that needs to be taken out. Which means assholes that need to be taken off this earth that don't play by our rules, and this is our secret playground.

"Are you ready?" Leo asks when I stop in front of Joker who is tied to the chair; head covered with a black hood.

I shuck off my shirt and hoodie so I have something I could go back home in.

"For her, I'm always ready, and this piece of shit will find out his mistake in touching what is mine. Do you have my stuff?"

"I thought so, and yeah, we have it right here." He pushes a tray, and Aiden unwraps the set of surgical tools. "It's all here. We will be standing right over there." He points behind me.

Mase walks backward toward the guys standing in line. "Let us know if you need us."

"Are you ready to die?" I remove Joker's gag.

"Fuck you, you piece of shit," he spits. "You can kill me. You can torture me but I got to taste and fuck what you love the most. Her."

I punch him in the face and hear the crunch when I break his nose.

He laughs and spits blood on to the concrete floor. "At first, I thought you didn't care for her but the way you looked at her when her brother wasn't looking, it was too easy to figure out that you fucked her. The best part of it all was the look in her eyes when she came to the house looking for you." He pauses and leans back. "I knew something was up and it was obvious she was holding something in her hand and she thought no one was there, but I was. It was a pregnancy test, and you were fucking someone else in the room just like you did when she moved here."

It feels like a knife is twisting in my chest. I could have prevented it if I wasn't so hellbent on trying to forget her. I've hurt her in so many ways. Because of my actions, and who I am.

I grip him by his greasy hair and pull hard so he can look at me. "How do you know what I did when she moved here?"

"Do you think I didn't know where she was all this time? I have to tell you; her pussy was good when I fucked her in the bathroom of the restaurant sh—"

I don't let him finish. I rain blows over his face until my arms feel like lead, but I need to stick to the plan. Inflict pain and leave him for two days to let him feel what she felt. Pain. He will understand the meaning of the word. All the years of pain bottled into six days of torture.

My arms feel heavy after beating him, his face is a battered mess and he's wheezing. "Laugh now, die later, cabron. I'm going to kill you nice and slow. The same way you tried to break what I love the most, but you underestimated her. You underestimated my love for her, but you also overlooked one thing; you fucked with a woman who belongs to the Cortez Cartel and we don't like when you touch our women. We don't like rapists or human trafficking sicarios."

"You think...they will let you kill me," he says, struggling on the last part.

"Who is going to protect you when there are five Cartel families you have disrespected. This isn't about the organization you work for; this is about me and you, pendejo." He doesn't know about Linda. He doesn't realize how many people he fucked with. "My son is the nephew of the Italian mafia's Goddess, puto. You thought Alina was some hyna I don't care about? A son you manipulated and let everyone think he belonged to you while his mother lived in fear while you degraded her and blackmailed her in being your whore. You beat her and I saw the pictures of what you did. The videos you used to blackmail her. The surgery you made her get to make her into what you wanted her to be but you forget she's mine. She always was and she always will be." His eyes widen when I pick up a set of pliers. " It was a clever move, but sangre es sangre. Blood is blood. It calls when it spills and it always wins. Love always prevails. In the good and in the bad. That is what makes her so special. She can fuck a pathetic dirty motherfucker like you, take the beatings, the degradation, but she was protecting me. Protecting the truth of our love. Our son." I lower my head and look at his mangled face. "She didn't break. She survived and deep down she knew I would come for you. My son called for me because there is no way he knew you were good for her. See, you don't understand that part of me lives in him. You can't break me. You could never break her. Now I'm going to break you for trying."

For the next two hours. I remove all his teeth and fingernails, relishing in his screams. Revenge is part of the suffering.

The pain passed on.

Transferred like energy.

Evil is not created; it exists inside us, and when it is unleashed, it is never forgotten.

Forty-Seven

ALEX

I wash my hands for the tenth time, not wanting to touch my family with dirty hands. Joker was screaming like an animal as he got slaughtered until he went quiet in shock.

The guys were surprised I didn't finish him off, but I wanted his wounds to drip. The pain to pulse.

So I can continue the second day and start all over on another part of his body.

I walk into Maxim's room and find it empty. I frown and walk to the bedroom, relieved to see him snuggled with his mother.

She's the best feeling in the world.

There is nothing like the scent of her skin and hair.

Knowing my son, he saw his mother sleeping alone and he wasn't having it. Good job, Maxim. It's funny how his instinct is to protect and make her feel loved and important. Sometimes, we think parents are supposed to teach their kids, but our kids teach us.

They show us what we can't see.

The signs were all there, I was too blind to see it.

I sleep for two hours and then get up to make my future wife and my son breakfast.

"Where were you?" Alina asks.

I raise my brow, silently reminding her of the other day when I asked her the same question but I tease her instead, "Missed me?"

She looks at Maxim scarfing down his pancakes while he watches his favorite show and then her eyes land on mine. "Are you trying to get back at me?"

"No."

"I expected an answer, but I respected the fact that you weren't willing to tell me. I don't want you to think I am holding you hostage."

"I'm here because I want to be."

Thank fuck.

We're interrupted by the sound of the doorbell. I check the door camera and close my eyes. Joaquin.

When I open the front door, a fist flies and connects with my jaw.

"*Hijo de mierda*! I won't say your mother because she doesn't deserve her memory thrown in the mud. But my sister! I had one rule and you broke it! You stuck your disease-infested cock in her!" Joaquin yells, and Maxim and Alina run down the hallway.

"Uncle Joaquin! Don't hit my daddy!"

I hold my hand up to let him know I'm okay.

"Joaquin! What the hell are you doing!" Alina yells.

"Not letting him use you like he does all the others. I trusted him with you. I trusted him!" He seethes in anger.

She gets in front of him when he tries to lunge at me. "Stop it! You're upsetting Maxim."

Maxim is covering his ears and his eyes are shut. I pick him up and his eyes snap open. "It's okay, Maxim. Daddy is here. I'm okay. Uncle Joaquin is upset, that's all," I coo.

"He hurt you, Daddy," he says with a frown. I grimace when he touches the spot.

"I'm okay, hijo."

When I look up, Joaquin is looking at me with a murderous glare. His lip curls, and honestly, I was prepared for his reaction. "Did you know?" He means about Maxim. "Di–"

"He didn't until recently," Alina interjects. "Stop acting crazy."

"When?"

Alina rolls her eyes, pointing at Maxim in my arms. "Do the math. I know you're not that stupid."

"Why didn't you tell me?"

I look at Maxim and say, "Maxim, go to your room. Me and your Uncle have to talk." He nods and runs off.

I walk over where Joaquin is towering over his sister in a fit of anger. I push him away. "Be careful, *ese*. I let you punch me once, but don't corner her. Don't upset her."

He laughs maniacally. "Oh, I'm the enemy now? You're going to kick my ass, *pinche pendejo*, huh?"

I pull Alina and lower my voice in a lethal tone. "Don't you ever question or scream at her. I've killed people for less."

He knows I'm not fucking around. Alina looks at me nervously, not knowing what to do.

He calms down and rakes his fingers through his hair. "Do you love him, Alina?"

My heart rattles inside my chest. What if after everything, she realizes that she can't love a man like me.

"I've loved him since I was seventeen." She blinks back tears, and my heart slams. "It doesn't matter if I'm beaten or blackmailed. Even if I try to forget him, I still love him and I always will.

I pull her into my chest and hold her tight. She sobs into my chest. "I love you, too. You're it for me, Alina," I say softly. I look up over her head at my best friend. "I'm sorry for keeping it from you and because of that, I hurt her without knowing what my actions would cause. I'm not letting her go and there is no one that is going to take her from me, again. It's her and Maxim, Joaquin. They're my family. And she's the love of my life."

"You know what this means, *ese*. Does she know what being with you means for her and Maxim?"

"She's my queen and my son is the heir to the Cortez Cartel."
"Yeah, they're targets, Smiley."
"They have to get through me and the Kings first."
"And Joker?"
Alina pulls away, and her eyes dart to me and to her brother, waiting for me to respond. "I'm taking care of it."
"How?"
"I'll show you."

Forty-Eight

ALEX

"You're marrying my sister?" Joaquin asks on our way to the warehouse.

"If she says, yes."

"You haven't asked?"

I tap my thumb on the steering wheel and turn into the parking lot. Once parked, I open the glove compartment and pull out a black velvet box. I hand it to him and sit back and wait until he opens it.

He looks at the ring for a minute in silence. I give him a moment and then I ask, "I haven't asked her yet because I need you to do me a favor."

He sniffs, closing it and gives me a choked up, "What is it?"

"I need you to walk your sister down the aisle. Do you think you can do that? It will mean a lot if you give her to me. I'll protect her and give her everything."

"What about the Kings in the east? Who will run them?"

"You will. I have to take over for my father and remain here with the Kings in the West and raise my children because I plan on having more with my wife."

He places the tiny black box inside the glove compartment. "What about Lucy? Do you still love her?"

"I love Lucy as my cousin's wife and a friend. I thought I was in love with Lucy, but Alina is my soulmate. My wife. The mother of my child. She stole my heart the first night I made her mine. She took everything good and look what she created."

"The most beautiful human, Maxim."

"She created something only God can give, brother. It makes me human. Alina reminds me that I'm worth something and not the monster my father destined for me to be. I'm not the gangster, the cholo, or the cartel king. With her, I'm a husband, a father, an uncle, her lover, and her protector."

"She means that much to you, huh?"

"Yeah."

He opens the door of the car. "I'm not sorry for punching you in the face, *cabron*. You deserved that shit."

I open the door to the warehouse. "Fuck you, *ese*. You hit like a pussy."

Skinning a person alive in our world is like deleting their story from existence. Your *placa* is a sign of honor when you initiate in a gang. Having it taken from you is a dishonor. Giving him a quick death is like a painless one.

Joker laughed at first, screamed after, and then pleaded for mercy.

Joker died from pain and shock after I cut his penis and balls off. He watched himself bleed out. The last thing he saw when his eyes rolled back in his head was my smile and heard my last words. "Who's laughing now, pendejo."

Forty-Nine

ALINA

"How has everything been going?" I ask Julio when I walk in his office Monday morning after dropping off Maxim.

"I should ask you the same. Your brother was here."

"Was he?"

Why would Joaquin show up at the shop to see Julio?

"You guys close?"

He shakes his head, looking over an invoice. "No, he asked why you kept coming here."

I swallow nervously. "What did you say?"

"Alex has known you have been coming here. You know that, right? He can't see inside here but he knows where you've been going."

"But he asked me and I didn't say anything."

"He doesn't want you to feel like he's controlling you. I think you've had enough of that in your life, Alina. He wanted you to feel like you have a choice to come and go. Make breakfast for your son like he likes and take him to school and do whatever it is that makes you happy."

"Why didn't he say that he knew or get mad."

Julio gives me a genuine smile. "Maybe, he wanted you to choose, but you came back to him every day."

I did have enough money to leave. I could have left with Maxim. I had the car and the money.

"He would have let me go?"

"Yes, but he would have followed you. "

"What about the Kings? He wouldn't leave them."

Julio chuckles. "He already did. Joaquin is taking over. He did it for you, Alina. He wants to be whatever you want him to be."

"But that's his identity."

"You're my identity." My head whips to the office door. Alex walks in and tilts his head to the side. "Have lunch with me?"

My eyes find Julio and he smiles , "He owns the shop, Alina."

"But I thought—"

"I'm part owner, but he owns the majority of the shop. He's been paying you."

Alex pulls me toward his chest, and I close my eyes and breathe him in. "You can still work here if you promise to dance for me like you agreed to."

"You still holding me to that?"

"Hell yes. I can't resist watching you. If it weren't for Maxim, I would put a pole in the apartment."

I have a feeling he would.

I stare at his handsome face. "Yes, I'll have lunch with you."

♛

I follow him outside and see a classic 1964 Chevy Impala.

Alex holds the door open for me.

"Ride with me?"

"Like old times."

"Like old times when we were seventeen. You and me. Ride or die, eh?"

He took me to a meet up in L.A., in his first car. He was so excited when he got it. He ran in the house and he looked at me and pulled me outside and opened the door just like this. Wait. "Is this—?"

"The same one."

"You kept it."

"I restored it and kept in the garage. When Julio showed up, he said he could restore it. It's been here ever since."

I admire the candy red paint with the mural. It's a classic. La Cultura.

I press a soft kiss on his lips. "I love you."

"I love you, too."

When I move to slide inside, I place my hand on the seat and blink hard. There is a tiny black box. I grab it and stand, turning to face him. My heart is beating in my throat. My stomach fluttering.

"Alex," I say on a whisper.

"This first time I saw you I knew you were different. It was as if time stood still, and in that fleeting moment, I knew deep inside that you held a special place in my life. You effortlessly embodied everything that is pure and beautiful, illuminating my world even in the midst of my own flaws and imperfections. That contrast, that dance of light and darkness, is what makes our connection truly meaningful." He takes my hand and opens the box and the huge diamond glitters from the light of the sun. "Marry me, Alina. You and Maxim. Be mine forever because I can't imagine a life without you."

Tears slide down his cheeks, and my heart somersaults. "Yes," I say softly.

He lifts my chin. "I promise to be there and love you, *Princessa*."

He places the ring on my finger, and I stare at it the whole way to the small restaurant. I can't stop looking at it. I'm engaged.

My phone goes off, and I open the group call. "Please tell me you said yes, he's been driving me crazy," Lucy says.

"For real, he's been driving us fucking nuts," Mase adds.

"I know, right. We told him you loved him but he was so scared.

He cried thinking you were going to tell him no," Katalia says, rolling her eyes.

"Did you tell him?" Linda asks, and I widen my eyes.

"Tell me what?" Alex asks, glancing at me.

"I'm taking that as a no," Linda responds.

"What is it? I'm nosy," Aiden chimes in.

I roll my eyes. "You guys suck. I can't tell you all shit. I just asked for one day." I take a deep breath and look at Alex. "I'm pregnant," I announce.

Alex slams the brakes and pulls over. "Say that again, *Princessa*."

I laugh. "I'm pregnant. I missed my period and took a test. It's positive."

"Yes! More baby shopping," Lucy says in excitement, and the guys groan.

"Mase, do something. She bought us each a four-thousand-dollar stroller," Colton complains.

"*Orale*," Leo says. "Lucy, you need to chill. We don't have room for all this stuff."

"I want all the babies to look cute. Now we have to get Alina and Alex's baby the same stuff."

"We're going to have a daycare," Leo says.

"Oh, wedding is in my house."

"Whose house?" Alex asks, not hearing Aiden because he's driving back on the road.

"My house," Aiden says. "Khalani's pregnant and she wants to play matchmaker."

"Arranged marriages are old school. What if they hate each other?" Leo asks.

He has an agreement with Niko's father, Dimitri.

"We hated each other and look at us now...We're married," Khalani chimes in.

Fifty

ALEX

One Month Later

"I do."

"You may now kiss the bride."

I lift her veil, and Alina smiles back at me.

"Congratulations, Mr. and Mrs. Alex Cortez."

Clapping and catcalls can be heard from our friends and family. I look to the sky and say a prayer in my head. Thank you, Mom. For bringing her back to me.

Alina wraps her arms around my waist. She's wearing a gorgeous mermaid style dress, and it's molded to her frame. Her stomach still flat. Soon. "What are you thinking about?"

I look over at the pool house, remembering the guys used to take girls there in high school to fuck. "Can you get out of that dress?"

"Why?"

"I think we should beat our kids to it while we can. The pool house."

She closes her eyes like she's thinking really hard and opens them. "It's not our house."

"I want to have sex with my wife."

"Take me in the Impala."

"You want me to fuck you in the Chevy?"

She nods, biting her lip." I hoped you would the first time you took me for a ride in it."

"I would have but I wasn't sure you were down for me."

"As you can tell, I am always down for you."

Her tits swell when she breathes, and my cock hardens under my pants. I pull her so she can feel what she does to me. "Alina, I want to come all over you in your wedding dress. I want to ruin you."

"Then what the fuck you're waiting for, *ese*. You're going to kick with me or what, eh?"

"As you wish, Mrs. Cortez."

"I love when you call me that."

"You look beautiful in your dress today. To me, you're the prettiest."

I feel a tug on my pants. I bend down and Maxim says softly, "Did you tell her, Daddy?"

"Yes, Maxim. I told her."

"Every day. Don't forget," he whispers.

I nod at Linda. She grips Maxim's hand, and I wink at her when I push Alina toward the entrance of the house. "I'll be right back."

"She's pregnant already, *ese*," Colton says.

"I know, but I have the rest of our lives to make memories. And I'm just getting started."

The End.

Thank you to all of you that loved the Hillside Kings as much as I did writing it. I hope you loved Alex and Alina. I know it feels like the end but more is coming.

The second generation is coming 2024!

Entre Familia: The Cartel Kings Series
Preorder is available for The Cartel Kings book one: A Dark High school Romance.
Releases 1/16/2024
Scan my QR code on the next page to preorder.

About the Author

Carmen Rosales is an emerging Latinx author of Steamy, and Dark Romance. Join her VIP list and Newsletter- www.carmenrosales.com

She loves spending time with her family. When she is not writing, she is reading. She is an Army veteran and is currently completing her Doctorate Degree in Business and has the love and support of her husband and five children. She loves to see a review and interact with her readers.

Follow her on Social Media and stay up to date with her new releases:

Acknowledgments

I would like to thank all my readers and new readers for purchasing my book. I hope you liked the fifth book in the series.

From the bottom of my heart, thank you.

I would like to thank my editors, beta readers, bloggers, ARC readers, book cover designer and CandiKanePr. Thank you for everything.

Book cover and logos by 3Crows Author Services